I0822492

LIES THAT BLEMISH

THE EMBER WAR SERIES
BOOK 3

LEIA STONE

Cover by The Illustrated Author Design Services.

This edition is published by Leia Stone LLC.

For Alie Rae. Every time a heart breaks, it mends together stronger.

LUSKA

THE WALL

GOLDEN HILLS

CEDAR CREEK

AMERSEA

THE COVE

RIVERINE

Imbria
The Wilds

CHAPTER
ONE

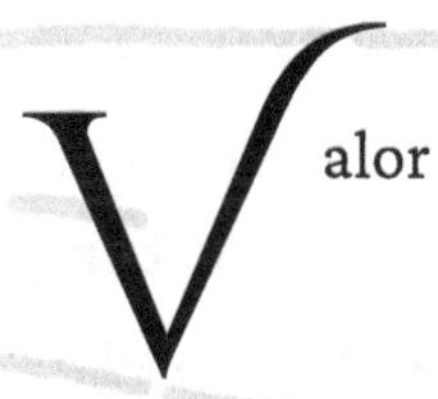alor

TWO MONTHS HAD PASSED since my sister, Aisling, the empress, declared war on Imbria. Now I stood at the mouth of the Wilds, staring at the smoke in the distance. The smoke of Imbria. Our country was burning. Theirs was, too. For every bomb they sent, we sent three more.

The only saving grace was that the war with Luska seemed to have turned cold now that Aisling had killed Prime Leader Vlek. But I knew that wouldn't last. My sister might be next, and as the heir, I had to bond a powerful creature today, or I was dead. And Virtue and Victory were right behind me.

A lump formed in my throat, but I swallowed it down. Everharts didn't cry.

Elaine swam into view, all hard lines on her face, but her eyes told the true story. She was worried for me. As she should be. Aisling trained her whole life to enter the Wilds, and to a certain degree, so did my sisters and I, but not as hard as she did, nor as ruthlessly. Elaine had been softer on us. She probably assumed we'd have time for a childhood. An assumption dashed the night Kohen Badshah killed our father. He was a cold and unforgiving man, yes, but the only parent we had—except for the woman standing before me.

"Green flares every hour to tell us you are alive. Red flare for evacuation." Elaine's voice shook as she reminded me of the rules the admirals had set forth. Bonding a creature at fourteen was unheard of, and they didn't want me getting any help from my sister or some security detail. If I did, then no one would follow me one day if I became empress. I had to prove I was strong enough on my own.

"Except when I'm sleeping—"

"You're *not* sleeping." Aisling stepped up and shoved a small satchel at me. If Elaine looked scared, Aisling appeared terrified. She cast frantic glances at our family car as if imagining sneaking me to safety.

"Not for the first forty-eight hours, obviously," I said, reciting her advice back to her, "but if I go into day three—"

"Stars, don't let her go into day three." My eldest sister looked up at the fire sky as if begging the stars to have mercy on me.

I'd overheard her talking to Elaine a few weeks ago. They

said at first they'd wanted me to bond in order to keep me safe, but now they thought it was a good idea because there was a very real chance Aisling would die before I turned nineteen, the age of the Lottery, and being bonded would make me look fit to rule. I'd overheard conversations in the last two months that had aged me ten years. Aisling died two months ago when Kohen killed her and was able to be reborn because of her creature's powers, but she and Elaine weren't sure she would come back again.

"...if I go into day three, I take a small nap to make sure that my fighting accuracy is still good," I finished reciting and then held the satchel up to my nose and inhaled.

Coffee.

Yuck.

I wasn't allowed coffee normally. I tasted Father's one time and spit it out onto the table. Elaine had made me clean it up myself, even though our maid was standing right there. My sisters had laughed the entire time.

I felt empty without Victory and Virtue beside me. I'd never slept a single night away from them in my entire fourteen years. We'd left my little sisters at home. They'd both been crying messes, and it would have broken me to have them here to say goodbye. This was bad enough... but better.

"She's going to be fine!" Tetra snapped, walking over to where I stood as she leaned on her cane for support. Her stunning wolf creature, Ariyel, strode alongside her. "Remember when you thought the Wilds would eat *me* alive?" she asked my sister.

Aisling didn't look like that comment made her feel any

better, but it made me grin. Tetra pulled me into a hug, and I squeezed her back. She was like a second older sister to me. I had no memories without her in my life.

Tetra pressed her lips against my ear. “Don’t go for anything crazy. A fox or wolf is good enough. Get in, get out, get home alive,” she told me and then backed away.

I nodded to her. It was solid advice, but also… was it enough? It used to be. But now Aisling had a Talanagi. Would my people now expect that of all empresses and emperors to come?

It didn’t matter. It wasn’t like finding a Talanagi was easy.

“I’m ready,” I declared, my hand resting on the custom serrated blade Aisling had given me. I felt like I was going to throw up, but I kept my chin held high.

“No,” Aisling said suddenly, and then looked at Elaine. “We didn’t train her long enough. I was busy with the Imbrian war. Let’s wait.”

Aisling reached out and grasped my shoulders, looking me dead in the eyes. “I’m calling this off.”

I growled in her face, an animalistic sound. “Don’t you dare!” I snapped.

Tetra and Elaine walked away to where two Fleet guards were standing near the entrance, giving us privacy. “This is the only thing giving me peace, Aisling,” I told her. “You’re never around anymore. Gwen is great, but what if something happens? What if Vic or Virtue is taken? I can protect them with a creature.”

She had no idea the nightmares that tormented me since

that freak Maxim had mailed our hair ribbons to her. I heard Elaine say he was probably stalking us. No way was I leaving without a creature!

Aisling released a shaky breath and met my gaze. I didn't remember anything about my mother, but I'd seen pictures, and staring at my sister now, I could see my mother's face in Aisling. She was beautiful and sad.

"If you die, I'll die," she croaked.

I'd never seen Aisling as emotional as I had in the last few months. Growing up, she was always stiff as steel, like Father and Elaine. Then something happened, and now she was soft. She said *I love you* to us every time she saw us and looked on the verge of tears right now, which I'd never seen before in my life.

"Ash, it's me. The most *feral* of all your sisters. I got this." That got a grin out of her.

"What if you don't bond? What if you get hurt?" she said.

"What if I bond a ruthless bear creature and don't get a scratch on me?"

Aisling gave me a half smile. "You got my cockiness, and that is not a good thing."

"I'm going to be okay," I told her, my voice cracking a little. "I need this."

I swallowed hard as the vision of my dead father in the morgue rose in my mind. One day, he was strong, mean, normal, and the next... gone.

Aisling seemed to be having a mental battle of her own. I could see it in her eyes. She didn't want to let me go. She'd spent the past week in the countryside, flying in on Liana's back early evenings and sparring with me, trying to train me while flying back to base to tend to the war.

I peered over at the flaming hills of Imbria.

"Did you love him?" I asked her, and she bristled, eyes going wide.

"I overheard you and Elaine," I said.

Kohen, Father's killer, and Aisling were once an item. He'd wormed his way into her heart in order to get closer to Father. But the way she'd been acting the past two months, I wondered if it had been more than a fling.

"I thought I did," she said finally, but her voice was dead, devoid of emotion. She was shutting down, the Aisling I was used to.

"He or Maxim might get you next," I said.

She chewed on her lip, flicking her gaze my way. "You've been eavesdropping?"

I winced. "You talk loud."

She rolled her eyes. "I can rebirth."

"Not forever," I countered. "Ash, you gotta let me do this." I pulled her into a bone-crushing hug.

I didn't really know what love was. I'd once looked it up in the dictionary. *An intense feeling of deep affection, a strong emotional bond.* I had that with my sisters, with Aisling, with Elaine. I just didn't verbalize it. Father told us not to, that it was a weakness. Now I wondered...

"I love you..." I tried the words out, surprised at how easily they came.

Aisling pulled back, shocked, grinning. "I love you too, little sis."

I shook myself. "Okay, gross, that was way mushy."

Aisling laughed. "You're right. The little sis part went too far."

I shot her a smile, loving this banter and how normal we were right now. I missed this part of my older sister. We used to go back and forth like this all the time. Now, she was never around, and when she was, she was so serious.

The two guards came to escort me to the entrance, and Aisling stiffened.

"I got this," I winked at her, ignoring the terror ripping through me at the thought of spending two, possibly three, nights in the Wilds alone.

She just nodded as Tetra and Elaine flanked her, and their creatures stood behind them. Liana was behind Aisling and nodded once to me. I nodded back. My sister's creature and I had grown close the past few weeks. She let me pet her neck and ask questions about the Wilds to her through Aisling. I think she liked me.

I took one last look over my shoulder, then sucked up every ounce of fear I had and shoved it deep inside of myself to a place I refused to deal with for the next three days.

It was time to bond a creature, by *any* means possible.

CHAPTER TWO

Aisling

WATCHING my little sister walk into the Wilds alone in the middle of a war was the hardest thing I'd ever done. I wanted to run after her, drag her back to the car, and drive away with her where I could keep her safe. But that would do nothing to help our situation long term, which was worsening by the day. Since the last letter Maxim sent, which stated he would give me three months to submit to his insane demands, Luska had gone eerily quiet on the war front. Which was a good thing because I was fighting that traitor Kohen every second I got. It also meant I only had one month left to get our fleet strong enough to pummel Luska so that Maxim could never follow through with his threat—to kill my sisters and take my lands if I didn't marry him and relinquish my country.

Just thinking of that bastard's letter made my blood boil, but not as hot as Kohen's betrayal. My heart still ached somehow, even though it was currently a pile of ashes inside my chest. Kohen killing my father, admitting it, and then killing me was enough to deaden me inside.

'Valor will be okay,' Liana said into my mind. *'She's strong. Stronger than you know.'*

I tried to take solace in Liana's reassurance, but it felt empty, as empty as I was inside. Elaine and I had argued for two weeks back and forth about giving Valor a map and information about where the Talanagi were in the hopes she could bond one. But in the end, we both decided against it. She was fourteen, for crying out loud! And emotional. She screamed in anger during drills and growled and grunted her way through sparring practice. She wasn't focused like I was. She wasn't ready. We had to hope she would bond a lion or a wolf or something decent. Then we had to pray my people would follow her if I died.

'Who would employ a lamb as a guard after having a bear?' Liana asked me.

She was on team, "Give Valor a map to the Talanagi." Liana and I were at odds a lot lately.

'You think because I've now set the bar of being empress with a firebird, that my sister will have to have an equivalent creature to rule?' I asked her.

'I do.'

Damn. I hated her advice. It was harsh and out of my control now.

'Well, then... I'll just have to live and reign forever,' I snapped, walking away from her and over to Elaine and Tetra.

They both spoke in hushed voices and quieted when I came near.

"She's going to do great," Tetra said.

"Absolutely," Elaine said.

They were both acting fake so that I wouldn't crack. That much was clear.

I glared at the guards. "I wish the admirals would have permitted me to fly over and at least track her."

Elaine nodded. "That's special treatment, something you never had. She has to prove she's fit to lead this country."

She wasn't, though! Not yet. She was a child who'd barely just started her period. I hated that my father's death had propelled us all into roles we weren't ready for.

And that was Kohen's fault.

Sometimes at night I went crazy, replaying some of the insanely romantic things he said to me. But lately, it was this: *I'll burn this entire world down before I let a hair on your head be harmed.* He said that before he had someone blow a poison dart into my body and kill me!

I wanted to cleave his head from his shoulders myself, but honestly, I wasn't sure I could do it.

"Come now. We have your engagement party to attend," Elaine reminded me.

I groaned.

Alek. Sweet and loyal Alek, who was marrying me for the good of our people. He was like a little puppy dog, always there waiting for my affection, which I had no intention of giving him. No, this was strictly business. I'd rather die than allow another man into my heart again. I'd learned enough about love to know that it wasn't for me. Not the romantic kind. Only love for Elaine, Tetra, my sisters, and Liana would last. And even that was a challenge at times. I thought of how Valor had just said those three words to me and smiled a little. I wasn't a parent, but I might as well be, and I was proud of myself for teaching my sisters that it was okay to say that. Something my mother had said all the time and my father had poisoned.

'People who can't love, who have no empathy for others, they scare me,' Liana said.

My gaze flicked to where she stood. *'Are you talking about my father?'* I hated it when she intruded on my thoughts. *'He wasn't incapable of love. He just didn't like to say the words,'* I told her.

She didn't respond. I didn't like how Liana and I had been at odds over things lately. I normally wanted to hear her opinion and guidance on everything, but where Kohen and my father were concerned, we disagreed. She thought there might be something to what Kohen said about my father and that I should find him and question him further, but I knew better—I knew better than to let his beautiful lips utter any more of their poisonous lies. If I let him speak, I'd probably fall under his spell and believe whatever he said. *No.* I didn't trust myself where he was concerned.

The facts remained: he admitted to killing my father, and that was punishable by death.

I slipped onto Liana's back, and we headed for Riverine to my engagement dinner, where all of the high society mucky mucks would be watching me. They wanted me to have a strong husband by my side, someone loyal to the capital. And that's what I was going to give them.

They already thought I was a failure for losing half of our country to Imbria. I wasn't about to have a coup on my hands. I'd smile and dance and hold Alek's hand. Whatever kept my head on my neck and my sisters safe.

CHAPTER THREE

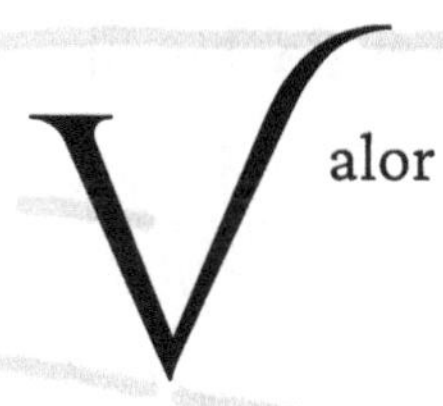

alor

Ember was beautiful, like a raining fire. I watched it dance down to the forest floor and burn there, smoking against the cool moss. I should probably grab a chunk. It was practically a rite of passage, but considering my sister was the empress and, therefore, the richest person in the country, it felt wasteful. I'd leave it for the embersmiths to mine or the next Lottery candidates.

A twig snapped to my right, and I spun that way, dagger out. A small little ferret with purple ember marks raced along the forest floor, and I let out the breath I'd been holding.

Okay, Valor, a little jumpy.

I took a deep breath and rolled out my shoulders, trying to relax. If my sisters were here, I might feel better—I wasn't used to being alone. Being a triplet meant I'd *never* been alone, not even in the womb. But if they were here too, I'd also be worried about them and constantly looking out for them. No, this was better. If anything horrible happened to me, they wouldn't see it. And in three days, the guards would find my body and bring it back—

No. Stay positive. You're getting out of here alive, I told myself.

It was hard not to have negative self-talk. I had an inner voice sometimes that hated me, and it sounded a lot like Father's voice.

No, not like that, Valor.

You're not doing it right, Valor.

That's not good enough, Valor.

Aisling is better at that than you are, Valor.

You need to try harder, Valor.

Sometimes, I wondered what magic he had over Aisling that she idolized him so much. I mean, I was pissed that Kohen Badshah murdered him; sad to officially be an orphan... but I wasn't mad he was gone. The nights were peaceful, the days without constant scrutiny. Now, I was just terrified that my older sister would be next. Someone I actually cared about and would be devastated to be without.

Where my mother's death left a hole, and Father's cold, hard neglect grew that hole ever wider, Aisling filled it. Along with Elaine, I had a vivid memory of baking cookies in the kitchen at seven years old, and a then-twelve-year-old Aisling picked up a hunk of raw dough and threw it at me. Father had been yelling at me earlier for not paying attention to my studies, and I was in a rotten mood. I had spun to her, angry, only to see her smiling before she threw another chunk. What erupted next was the first and last food fight we'd ever had. My sisters and I clobbered Aisling with cookie dough until she was laughing on the floor, and we rubbed it into her hair.

When Elaine came in, I thought she'd kill us all. But Aisling took the blame. My big sister.

I couldn't let anything happen to her, which was why I needed to bond the biggest, most powerful creature possible so that I could protect Victory, Virtue, and even Aisling, too. My big sis was so busy running the country that she barely took care of herself. She'd lost weight. I barely saw her eat. She drank coffee constantly, and she was consumed with the war and making Imbria pay for what they did.

Another twig snapped, and I spun, sucking in a breath, and I saw two Imbrian boys, one about my age, one a little older. Like me, they wore packs and had swords on their hips, but they didn't look like soldiers. They had soot in the creases of their skin like they'd gone through the burning fields to get here.

I held my blade aloft. "You're on the wrong side of the border," I spat.

We were at war with the Imbrians again. That meant this was our side, and across the river was theirs. They were probably just here to steal ember but it was *our* ember, not theirs.

"Valor Everhart?" the eldest said, and my stomach dropped.

No.

Assassins? I hadn't prepared for this. Without giving it a second thought, I reached into my thigh holster with my free hand and pulled a throwing star. With one flick of my wrist, it sailed past the older boy's head and sliced the tip of his ear right off.

With a scream, both boys crouched to the ground, putting their arms out in surrender.

"Holy crap, she tried to take my ear off!" the older boy said as he cupped his bleeding ear and glared up at me.

"I was actually trying to take your eye, but close enough," I snarled, stalking forward with my dagger raised.

The younger boy who had been quietly watching me stood then, stepping in front of his elder brother, and held up his hands as I pressed the tip of my dagger to his chest.

Stars, he was gorgeous. His eyes were crystalline blue, and even though he had a baby face, it was still chiseled.

"Kindly go back to your lands, or I'll carve out your heart with my sword," I told him.

He frowned. "You have everything wrong, Valor."

The way he said my name, like he knew me. "Did you come to kill me?" I asked, wondering how he knew who I was. Aisling was always well known as Father's heir, but my younger sisters and I were lesser known to Imbrians.

"I'm Arjun. Arjun Badshah," he said, and I sucked in a

breath. His older brother stood, still glaring at me as he held a bandage to his ear. "That's Tej." Arjun flicked his head in his brother's direction. "Our brother Kohen sent us—"

"To kill me," I growled, pressing the tip of my dagger into his chest so that it punctured the cloth.

He took a step back, muttering a string of Imbrian that I could barely pick up—it was too fast. Something about... *beautiful demon*.

"We came to help you bond a Talanagi!" Tej screamed. "But there's no way in hell I'm helping you now." He hooked Arjun by the underarm and began to drag his brother away.

Confusion flushed through me.

Help me bond a Talanagi?

Arjun dug in his heels, ripping away from his brother. "No. Kohen said she would resist. Without us, she dies!" he argued with his elder brother, and at his declaration, cold, hard fear flushed through me.

Without us, she dies? How the hell would he know that?

"Yeah, I don't care." Tej indicated his bleeding ear.

Arjun nodded, yanking out a rolled-up paper that was peeking out from his brother's pack. "Then I'll help her." He turned back over to me and began to open the paper wide.

It was a map. I was so confused that I lowered my dagger, trying to make heads or tails of what was happening.

"She cut my ear!" Tej groaned.

Dammit, they didn't seem like very good assassins.

"I can cauterize it if you come over here." I lowered my dagger and my pack and began to rifle through for my med-kit. I had a small bit of gauze that, when activated with anything wet, turned to a glue-like putty. Aisling had to raise hell and search three army bases to get it for me.

Tej continued to glare at me. "If you think I'm ever letting you touch me, you're insane."

I rolled my eyes. "Fine. Suit yourself."

I shoved the med-kit back into my pack, picked up my dagger, and sauntered off into the woods.

"Would you both stop acting like children before she gets killed!" Arjun shouted, and I stopped.

There it was again. A threat to my life? I wasn't sure. He was speaking like he knew the future.

I turned, pulling my blade again. "I am heir to the empress' throne. If you have intel on a threat to my life, speak now," I warned.

Arjun looked at his older brother, who shook his head.

"Our brother Kohen can see the future," Arjun blurted out.

"You idiot!" Tej scolded him, going as far as to smack him in the back of the head. It made me smile a little, reminding me of my sisters, but the smile was erased quickly when I processed what he'd said.

"See the future? That's illegal." And a total lie, I was sure.

"I know, so that's why if you tell anyone, it will be big trouble for my brother. I'm trusting you—like Kohen told me I could," Arjun said.

Something about that softened my heart, but only for a fraction of a second. "Oh, your brother, *who murdered my father*, said you could trust me? That's cute." My voice was dripping with sarcasm.

Arjun frowned. "He killed that bastard to protect your sister, who he's in love with."

Chills raced along my arms, and my mouth popped open.

"She can't see reason. Don't bother," Tej snarled.

Arjun took another step closer to me, rubbing the spot where I'd cut a hole in his shirt. Was he bleeding? Kohen killed Father to protect Aisling? That made no sense. Except it might... if Father was going to kill her first.

Nausea roiled into me. "You're a liar," I told him, taking a step back. "He isn't in love with Aisling. He killed her, too!"

Arjun nodded. "To buy himself time to get to us, to get us into an underground bunker before she started bombing."

That made no sense. Why kill the one you love—? Then I remembered Aisling's confession to me. That she was basically immortal. Did Kohen know? Did he know she would rebirth?

My hand shook. "My father would never hurt Aisling." The lie tasted like poison on my lips.

Arjun frowned. "Okay... let's focus on the future, not the past. I have a map. It leads to where all the Talanagi are. Where your sister and my brother bonded Onyx and Liana."

Talanagi? Was he trying to get me killed?

"I don't have a death wish," I told him.

"You won't die. Not if you travel with us and we become one pack. Just for the next two days."

He spoke with so much confidence it was unnerving. "Two days?" I asked. "Why not three?" Three was standard.

"Because on the night of the second day, you will bond a

red dragon and fly yourself home. Safe. Alive. Powerful," Arjun said.

Shock. Greed. Desire. They all rolled through me in equal measure. A red dragon? It was my dream creature. He was lying. Playing on my desires. This was all a trap.

"What's in it for you?" I asked them.

Taj scoffed. "You're not the only one bonding Talanagi. We go together, we watch each others' backs, and we all go home bonded."

"You realize this sounds like a trap, and I'm not an idiot, right?"

Arjun nodded, pulling out a folded letter and handing it to me.

I opened it, scanning the contents.

Valor,

One day soon, you will be empress—

The first line took my breath away, and my heart skipped a beat. *No. Aisling...* I kept reading.

—for a short time while Aisling is... gone.

If you do not bond a Talanagi, your people will say you are too young and weak to lead. They will revolt, and the empire will fall. They will demand an elected leader, and your family's legacy will be over.

Holy crap. My heart hammered in my chest.

I know Aisling babies you, but I won't do that. The truth is, your father tried to kill Aisling at boot camp and had planned to do it again shortly after she would get her posting. I ended his reign to save her life, and I would do it again a hundred times over.

I love her, and by extension, that means I love you. You are important to her, so you're important to me. I need you to trust me. I've sent my most precious cargo to assist you. If you work together, I promise you all make it out bonded to Talanagi.

In the coming days, this will all make more sense.

Kohen

I stared at the letter in a complete stupor. Kohen Badshah just said he loved me. Not in a weird romantic way, but it was still weird and gushy and... what the hell! Father had plans to kill Aisling? Could that be true? I hated the fact that it made sense, that I could see him doing it...

"You okay?" Arjun asked.

I didn't want to think about this anymore. I warred with the decision. Go off on my own or team up with them? The chance to bond a Talanagi was too alluring.

"Just lead the way. I'm not sleeping, so if either of you comes for me, I won't hesitate to kill you," I said.

"Awesome," Tej mumbled.

I yanked out my med-pack and threw it at his chest. "You're welcome." But even as I said it, I felt bad. It was weird to have feelings that went against what you were taught. I was taught to hate the Badshah family, even more so lately after hearing my sister do nothing but speak day and night about how she was going to kill Kohen and avenge Father. Now, I was supposed to team up with his brothers? This was absolutely crazy. But also, if they wanted to kill me, they could have overpowered me by now. They hadn't even pulled their swords. Still, it felt like I was betraying Aisling.

But I needed the most powerful creature possible... so I was doing it.

After patching up Tej's ear, Arjun handed me back the kit.

"Where are the Talanagi?" I asked him.

Arjun flicked his gaze to his brother and then back to me. "Luska."

"Luska! Are you mad?"

"Scared?" Tej asked with a taunt.

I rolled my eyes. "I'm smart. I'm not going to enemy territory to bond a creature that might not even be there."

"Your sister did," Tej said.

Aisling went to Luska to bond Liana? *No way.*

"Enough talking. If we don't start now, we won't make it by the second night." Arjun waved us off and started walking.

Tej and I stared each other down. There was no way I was letting this guy have my back. We waited an agonizingly long moment before Tej groaned and then started to follow his brother. I pulled up the rear, telling myself this was an absolutely stupid plan and that I should turn back right now before I got in too deep with these two. Their extravagant lies were beginning to work on me because I was replaying every time I'd ever heard my father make a jealous remark at Aisling. Or the time I heard him tell Elaine she should have known better than to bond a Talanagi. Like, what did that mean? Why wouldn't he be proud of that?

Before I knew it, we'd been walking for an hour, and I had convinced myself they were right about Father. If there was a chance to bond a Talanagi and keep my sisters safe, I was taking it. No matter the risk.

CHAPTER
FOUR

isling

Alek leaned in to hug me and whispered into my ear. "You look stunning."

I wore an emerald-green dress that hugged my hips and was embellished with crystals along the neckline.

"Thanks," I told him as the attendant finished curling my hair and then left my dressing room. We were at the emperor's palace, my father's old place, where I grew up. We were about to take a car to a nice dining hall, where our engagement party was being held.

"Are you worried about Valor?" Alek asked. He was easy

to talk to. We'd become close friends over the past two months.

I nodded. "But my hands are tied. The second our party is over, I'm going back there to wait at the edge of the woods for her to come out," I told him.

"I can go with you. We could camp. Might be fun." He offered a handsome smile.

He was good-looking, sincere, sweet, loyal, and yet... I didn't have a burning fire for him inside of me like I had Kohen. I was ashamed of how deeply I'd allowed Kohen to infiltrate my heart. It felt like any "romance" that came after him would pale in comparison. And Alek kept hinting at wanting to go deeper with me, which I understood since, technically, we were engaged. But he knew this was a business arrangement.

I flicked my gaze to the tasteful gold band on my left hand, something small I could still fight with.

"Maybe," I told him. "You'd have to have your own tent," I added. We weren't married yet, and guards would be there. People would talk.

"Of course," he said, again eyeing my dress. "Aisling, I wanted to talk to you about something... delicate."

My gaze flicked up to his, roaming the strong lines of his face. His bright blond hair and blue eyes made him literally the opposite of Kohen in every way.

That should be a green flag right there.

"What is it?"

He cleared his throat. "Some rumors have started that our engagement is... a sham."

I shrugged. "I mean, it kind of is."

I regretted the words the second they left my lips.

Hurt crossed his face. He nodded, swallowing hard. "It may not be a love marriage, but our union will put faith into the hearts of the Amersean people that your reign will be long and full of heirs."

He was right. I needed to take this more seriously.

"Okay, what do you want to do? Pull up the wedding date?" I asked. I had learned Alek didn't bring up a problem without a solution. Something I really enjoyed about him.

He shook his head, taking a step closer to me. "No, we just need to act like we're in love."

It dawned on me then what he was suggesting. A kiss? A public kiss?

"My people know I'm cold and private, which is how a war leader should be. I'm not going to tongue kiss you in front of the entire country, Alek." Holding hands was enough to make me squirm. It was so showy.

Again, I couldn't help but notice the hurt that crossed his face, and my heart sank. He liked me. A lot. And I didn't feel the same. Which sucked harder than I thought it would.

"I would never suggest a crass tongue kiss, Aisling. I'm talking about something softer." He stepped closer again, and my heart began to race.

"With your permission, of course, I think once they announce us, we walk out holding hands and then... kiss. A small, delicate kiss that shows people we're in love. Even if we aren't."

He said that last part with a sorrowful tone, and it broke me.

I reached for his hand, pulling it into mine. "Alek, you can back out, you know. Find someone who adores you. You shouldn't have to be tied to me, knowing it's just an arrangement for the betterment of our country."

His eyes burned with passion then. "Even if this is the only way I can have you, as some arrangement, without your love, I'll take it, Aisling. For my country and for the small hope that maybe a decade in the future, you might soften towards me and reciprocate my love."

Love. He said *love*. His words had emotion clogging my throat. It was the sweetest thing he'd ever said to me, and I was painfully aware that we were still holding hands.

"Alek, what if I never feel the same? What if you spend your whole life just being... my friend?" Because I honestly wasn't sure I would ever love again.

He nodded. "You're worth the risk. And I'll have the adoration of whatever children we produce, that I'm sure of."

That made me smile. "Oh, you think our future children will love you more than me?"

He dropped my hand, nodding. "Of course. I'm the fun one, and you're the strict one. You say no to a second cookie, and the second you leave the room, I'm giving it to them."

"Alek!" I slapped his arm, laughing.

Stars, he was so easy to get along with. If someone could be trapped in a loveless marriage, it should at least be to their best friend.

"I do love you, you know?" I said, feeling bold.

He froze.

"As a *friend*. But... I do. I trust you, Alek, and I can count on one hand how many people I can say that about."

He nodded. "I appreciate that, and I intend to *never* betray that trust."

I just wished I could believe him. But Kohen had ruined that for me. Still, he was right. We needed to make the people believe our love was real.

"Yes, to the kiss when they announce us," I told him, and he swallowed hard.

"Okay. Should we practice before so it's not awkward?

"Are you an awkward kisser?" I asked in a teasing tone.

"No!" he scoffed. "I'm just saying it will be the first time we kiss. What if we bump noses and start laughing?"

I grinned. "You just want to kiss me, don't you?" I joked, and then felt bad for it.

His eyes flared to life. "Well, yeah, but not as a rehearsal for a play act."

Ouch, point taken.

"Okay, then kiss me." I shrugged, jutting out my chin and puckering my lips.

He peered at me with an intensity I hadn't expected. "Only psychos kiss with their eyes open," he scolded me.

I grinned, enjoying this banter, and closed my eyes, puckering my lips again. I expected to feel his lips on mine, but instead, he took the sides of my face gingerly in his hands, cupping my cheeks, and my heart raced. I hadn't been kissed since Kohen, and those kisses had been scorching, earth-shattering, soul-mending. I didn't feel that for Alek, so

I prepared myself for a kiss that felt dead, but when his lips pressed onto mine, ever so tenderly, a tiny spark ignited in my chest. A mild thrill went through me. But just as soon as it was there, he pulled away, and it vanished.

I opened my eyes, a little surprised to see him grinning.

"Dare I say you enjoyed that, Aisling?"

"Don't count on it," I told him honestly.

The door to my dressing room opened, and Alek stepped back a little. It was Admiral Elaine, wearing her full Fleet-issued suit. "There has been another letter," she told me and glanced at Alek.

I'd approved Alek to hear higher-level security clearance issues weeks ago.

I nodded that she could proceed.

"From Maxim?" My heart sped up. He hadn't written to me for two months.

Elaine shook her head.

Oh. Kohen. "Burn it with the rest of them," I said. He'd been sending a letter a week for two months now. They all said the same thing: your father was going to hurt you, I was saving your life, stop this fighting, and we will stop, blah blah.

Elaine cleared her throat. "This one is different... and you're going to want to read it alone."

Read a letter from Kohen? I hadn't done that in weeks. I'd stopped because it got hard, seeing his handwriting, hearing him plead with me to believe him. They were all the same, so I saw no point. He wasn't surrendering himself to justice, so I was going to keep going until we had him in handcuffs.

"I'll see you at the party," I told Alek.

He nodded, taking his cue to leave, and ducked out of the room.

Elaine strode over and handed me the letter, watching Alek leave the room.

"You didn't tell me Kohen could see the future," she said, and I bristled.

I snatched the letter from her hand and met her gaze. "Didn't seem to matter anymore."

She glanced at the letter. "I'll be waiting outside."

With that, she left the room. I'd given Elaine permission to read Kohen's letters and screen them for anything important, like a surrender. Otherwise, she was instructed to burn them. Had Kohen said in the letter that he could see the future?

I peeled it open and read.

Aisling,

Lately, I've learned something awful about my gift of seeing the future, and that is that the future can change. What used to be one road has now merged into two. Two possibilities, depending on what you do.

I froze, taking a shaky breath. Two futures? What was he talking about? I shouldn't even be reading these lies.

I see you married to Alek and me married to Anika. We are at peace in our own separate countries. You are decently content, having chosen duty over love. In this future, Luska is still a threat and you fight them until the day you die.

On the other possible road, I still see you as my wife. Our lands become one again, and we rule over them together, living out a happy life where Luska is no longer a problem. But it's a reality we will have to fight for, Aisling. You will have to fight for it.

You will have to be open to the fact that your father was a monster who tried to kill you and was—

I stopped reading because it went into the same old story, and I was starting to question my reality, my sanity. Could Kohen be right about my father? Stars, I hoped not. My heart ached at the thought of him marrying Anika, and then I hated myself for still caring. *He killed my father and then killed me!* Who cared if he knew I would rebirth. That was crazy. He was unhinged and, and... I needed to speak to someone who could give me unbiased advice. I felt my mind splintering at the edges.

'Young one, I promise you I am not taking his side, but I do think Kohen's claims deserve further investigation,' Liana said, and I groaned.

'I don't like your eavesdropping. I want to be alone!' I snapped at her and then immediately felt bad for it.

Who had I become?

My father. I was becoming my father: cold and uncaring, easy to anger. A single tear slipped down my cheek as I crushed the letter to my chest.

How many lies could you hear before it started to sound like the truth? Especially when they came from the lips of the one you once loved. My heart felt battered from the lies Kohen had burned into it time and time again.

'He sent a firebomb on our troops at the border today. How about I investigate that?' I asked Liana.

'After you sent one first,' she countered. *'He's just protecting his people. Notice he hasn't hit any civilian buildings, and casualties have been minimal.'*

I growled. *'Well, I haven't either.'* I'd been purposefully staying away from Sorak, the city I knew his brothers were in, because I was too soft to kill two young and innocent boys. But if Kohen was hiding out there, I would eventually have to storm the city and take it.

Liana sighed in my head. *'Aisling, you have both been fighting with minimal casualties. Can't you see this isn't a real war?'*

Her accusation that I was holding back because I still might love him, or that Kohen was doing the same, enraged me.

'He killed me, Liana. Watched as poison flooded my body, and my heart shut down. All the while whispering sweet nothings in my ear like a lunatic.'

She was silent because I knew she could say nothing after that cold, hard fact.

I tossed the letter into the fire and then left the room. I had an engagement party to go to and a people to convince that I was in love with Alek. The future of this entire empire rested on it.

CHAPTER FIVE

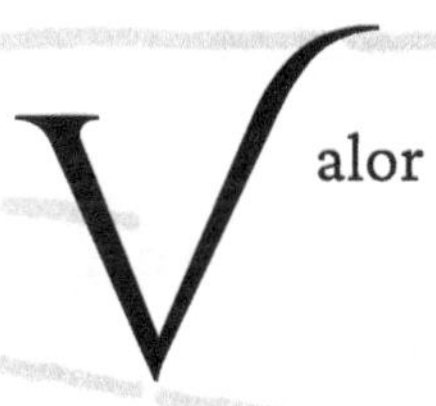

Valor

As the night grew longer, the boys slowed, yawning.

"Let's rest our legs for a bit," Tej said.

"I'm not sleeping," I declared as he set his pack down and rolled out his shoulders.

He pinned me with a glare. "Neither am I. I'm not an idiot."

"I'll sleep," Arjun shrugged. "That way, when you're both dragging, I'll be the most alert. Wake me when we leave." He yawned and pulled out his sleeping bag.

Tej and I shared a look, and we both tried to hide our smiles. Arjun was growing on me, but I still most definitely hated Tej.

A loud boom like a cannon rang out then, and I flinched, ducking my head. Tej and Arjun, who was getting into his sleeping bag, barely moved.

"Firebomb." Tej pointed up. I followed his gaze and saw a giant ball of fire streak across the sky from our side to theirs.

"You've never seen the battlefield, have you?" Tej asked in a somewhat disgusted tone.

"I'm fourteen," I huffed by way of answer.

Tej flicked his gaze to Arjun, who was now fully tucked into his pack. "He was a baby when your father took over our country. Age doesn't matter."

I rolled my eyes. "I don't want to waste my breath fighting, so if that's all you want to do, please be quiet."

"Oh snap," Arjun said from deep inside the sleeping bag.

Tej kicked him lightly. "Go to sleep," he growled at his brother.

But I smiled a little and then caught myself. We weren't friends. We had a mutually beneficial understanding, and that was it.

"I'm making a fire and some coffee," I announced.

After gathering some of the dry wood that was around us, I made a fire from the tinder and some matches in my pack. Then I started to boil water in a steel canteen I had.

Tej watched me with an annoyed expression that was really starting to piss me off. Another boom, and I flinched, and he did not. I peered up, praying it was a retaliation firebomb from their side. It wasn't. It was us. Again.

Tej pinned me with a glare, and I shrank under that gaze.

Why was Aisling burning half their country when they barely fought back?

Because Kohen killed Father and then her, I reminded myself.

Stay strong.

But by the time my coffee was brewed, another firebomb sailed over our heads from our side to theirs, and a pit formed in my stomach.

"Why aren't you fighting back? Don't you have an army?" I asked.

Tej glared at me. "Because my brother doesn't want to hurt Aisling. He loves her."

Love! Whoa. Just what in the hell had my sister gotten into with him? I didn't know, so I stayed silent and sipped the disgusting black coffee. It burned the back of my throat with a bitter tang.

Tej eyed the warm liquid, and I peered over at him.

"I don't want to toss this out, but I'm done. If you have a cup, you can have the rest," I said.

He didn't move for a moment, as if not wanting to take anything from me, but finally pushed off of the tree he'd been leaning on and pulled a steel cup from his pack. I filled the cup, and he muttered, "Thanks."

As he pulled it to his lips, I saw a blur of reddish fur behind him. Without thinking, I pulled my dagger and threw it, just as a large fox creature lunged from the woods and came for Tej. He saw me pull my blade and ducked just as my dagger sank into the creature's left eye. The fox yipped in pain, landing half on Tej's back and rolling to the ground before bolting into the woods.

Tej looked up at me with wide eyes, spilling coffee all over the ground. His hands shook, and my heart slammed against my chest. A soft snore came from Arjun's sleeping bag.

"Blood has been drawn," I said. "Do you think?" Once blood was drawn, a bonding started. You had to fight to the death or bond, and there was no way I was bonding a small fox creature.

"Go after it," Tej encouraged.

Without another thought, I bolted into the forest the way the fox had come and found it lying on the ground, struggling for its last breath.

It was incredibly sad, and suddenly, I didn't feel cut out for this. If Aisling were here, she'd pull the blade out of its eye and slice its throat to end its pain, but I wasn't Aisling. My dagger was embedded in its skull. To pull it out would be gross and traumatic. I... wasn't ready for this. All this blood and killing and torture.

There was no way I could bond a Talanagi by tomorrow night. I placed a hand on the fox's little chest just as it breathed its last breath, exhaling into the night. The red ember marks on its fur lit up brightly for a second before extinguishing. Tej had had no idea it was coming for him. It could have killed him. I was only trying to protect him.

I stared at the blade, unable to bring myself to pull it out.

Aisling would do it without hesitation, I told myself.

"Compassion isn't a bad thing," Tej said from behind me, and I stood, spinning.

When I could find my voice, I peered at the fallen fox. "That is my only weapon," I said.

Tej nodded, still seemingly in shock, and pulled a small dagger from the pack slung around his shoulder. It was almost identical in size to the one I'd lost. It was gorgeous, with a golden hilt and Imbrian engravings. He handed it to me, hilt first.

"Kohen said that would happen and to bring this for you. I... thanks for saving me," he said, seemingly in shock.

Kohen knew a fox would attack his brother, and I'd lose my dagger trying to help him? That I'd be too weak to pull it out of the dead creature?

What the hell?

I stared back at the dead creature. My blade was stuck so far into its eye that only the hilt showed. I didn't have the nerve to pull it out, which shamed me.

Turning back to Tej, I took the blade gratefully from him, sheathing it. "What else does he know?" I asked.

"A lot he won't tell me," Tej offered as we walked out of the thick brush and back to where his brother was still sleeping soundly. "He also said you won't tell anyone about his gift... so can you please keep it a secret?"

Keep a secret for an Imbrian? "I'll have to tell my sister, but no one else," I promised, still shaken by what had just transpired.

He nodded. "She already knows."

She did?

I sat back on my heels, blowing out a breath. How much did Aisling know and didn't tell me? She still treated me like a child.

Tej cast a wary glance over his shoulder. "Blood might attract the others. We should keep moving."

I sighed, nodding. He woke Arjun while I put out the fire and we kept heading north to the Wall. Did I just protect an Imbrian? Not just any Imbrian, but a Badshah? And why hadn't I retrieved my blade, the one my sister gave me, and was now instead carrying an Imbrian blade? I was going to look like a traitor.

But as I watched Tej ruffle Arjun's dark hair and call him silly names, I realized I didn't care. Hating Imbria was Father's thing, and now my sister's thing. But if Kohen's letter was right and Father had been about to hurt Aisling, then he did us a favor.

I wasn't going to live in the past.

CHAPTER SIX

Aisling

I PLAYED the role of the newly engaged bride very well. Alek and I held hands and even shared a public kiss, which sent the crowd wild with clapping. We ate and drank and danced as if our country weren't currently at war on two borders.

When it was all over, Alek was there, like a loyal puppy, asking again if I wanted his company to camp out at the entrance of the Wilds to wait for Valor.

I couldn't help but think of Kohen's letter.

I see you married to Alek and me married to Anika. We are at peace in our own separate countries. You are decently content, having chosen duty over love. In this future, Luska is still a threat and you fight them until the day you die.

I noticed he said you are decently content, having chosen duty over love. Not *we* are content. Did that mean he would regret marrying Anika for duty and heirs?

"I think I'd like to be alone, if that's okay," I told him.

He nodded as if he expected that.

"I had fun tonight," he told me, leaning forward to plant a kiss on my cheek. He gazed down at me, eyes blazing as if asking for more than a cheek kiss, and I stepped back a little. "Me too."

He nodded, looking a little dejected. "See you soon. Send word when Valor makes it out, so I don't worry."

Because he was an amazing guy and worrying about my sister who he knew was important to me. *Ugh.*

"I will," I told him, and then he left as I met Elaine outside with my packed duffle bag and got into our waiting car.

"Have you checked on the girls?" I asked. We'd moved them back in town when everything quieted on the Luska front. They were in the new willow tree house, and I requested to work out of Riverine as often as I could now that Sky Reach army base was basically dead. Luska wasn't fighting, which made me nervous. Were they building stockpiles? Preparing for a big hit? I didn't like the quiet. Half of our military was on leave, just waiting for orders.

The other half was in a watered-down war with Imbria.

"They're worried about Valor. Gwen is going to let them stay up late in case you send word."

Victory and Virtue had never slept a night away from Valor their entire life as far as I could remember. This would impact them all, and I hoped my sister was doing okay in the Wilds.

"Has Valor sent up any flares? It's been several hours."

Elaine nodded. "Green flares every hour. She's moving north."

Okay. That was good. I felt my body relax. "Let's camp at the northern entrance, then, and be ready to assess any injuries when she gets out."

Elaine relayed that to the driver, and we set off that way. Liana flew above us as Vespa curled up on the seat in front of us. It was already near midnight. We wouldn't reach the northern entrance to the Wilds for a few hours. I might as well sleep in the car.

Elaine lowered her voice: "Do you believe Kohen can see the future?"

I chewed my lip. "Yes."

She sat back in her seat and relaxed.

"Why do you look relieved?" I asked her.

She snapped her head in my direction. "Did you read his letter?"

"Not the whole thing."

Her eyes widened. "Aisling, he said at the very end not to worry about Valor, that she would bond a powerful creature and come out alive. That he's made sure of her safety."

Shock ripped through me, and I sat up straighter. "What?"

"Would he lie?" Elaine asked.

"Of course he would! He killed my father," I snapped. But it didn't seem like Kohen to randomly lie about my sister. Unless... I didn't ever really know Kohen in the first place.

"Probably not about this," I amended, feeling a little better myself. "What do you think he meant by him making sure of her safety?"

Elaine shook her head. "I don't know, but we've sent seven firebombs over the border since Valor stepped into the Wilds, and Kohen hasn't sent any back."

I frowned. "Stop sending them until she makes it out. Maybe that's what Kohen meant about keeping her safe. He's not going to fight us until she gets out."

Elaine looked honestly confused. "Why would he do that, Aisling?"

But she looked nowhere near as confused as I felt. If you were to look inside of me, I'd be twisted into knots. Nothing made sense anymore.

"I don't know."

'Because he loves you.'

'Funny way of showing his love,' I snapped back to Liana. I hated that we argued now.

"Can I ask you something, Elaine?" I peered at the woman who raised me.

She simply nodded. I glanced at the partition to make sure it was raised between us and Verik.

"Do you think my father would have hurt me? When I left for boot camp, you seemed like you wanted to tell me something. Like a warning."

Elaine's cheeks went pink, and she wrung her hands

together. Even Vespa perked her head up and peered at me. "Yes, I think he would have hurt you to keep you from getting more powerful than him, but I don't think he would have killed you like Kohen claims."

I was completely thrown by her answer.

"I'm his heir," I protested.

She nodded, meeting my eyes. "And there was nothing your father loved more than himself."

Ouch. But was she wrong? Even I would admit I was terrified to get a creature more powerful than him going into the Wilds, because I knew it would be frowned on by him. I was terrified of a lot when it came to my father, and I was just now questioning how normal that was.

"Hurt me how?" I asked her.

Elaine flicked her gaze to me again, appearing more nervous than I'd ever seen her.

"Elaine, if you know something—"

"I overheard him in his office... when you were in the Wilds. When word got back that you had perished, but that before doing so, you'd bonded a Talanagi."

I leaned forward so that I could be sure to hear every word.

"And...?"

She chewed her lip. "I wasn't eavesdropping. I'd been carrying a lot of the girls' laundry down the hall, and a bunch of socks slipped from my hands, and I had to bend down and pick them up—"

"Elaine, I don't care!" I told her.

"I heard him tell someone to 'Get the firebird and make sure she didn't bond.'"

I gasped, sitting back in my seat as her words sank into me. "You think he knew I would rebirth?" I asked her after a long time in silence.

We were on the highway now, trees passing by as we made our way north.

"I do. He had old books with knowledge in them of the Talanagi, and when he heard you bonded a firebird, I think he knew rebirth was possible."

No.

"Do you think he was behind Liana's kidnapping, to keep us from bonding and becoming too powerful?" I asked her, my heart racing in my chest. Why hadn't she told me any of this before!?

She pursed her lips. "I do. But I don't think he would ever kill you, Aisling."

Holy crap.

My breath came out in short bursts as Elaine squirmed next to me on the seat.

"You should have told me sooner," I said.

"I didn't think it mattered. Once you were bonded and off to boot camp, it wouldn't matter."

But it *did* matter.

"Elaine, the men holding Liana that night had Marble Shore accents. But then, when we got attacked at the train during our boot camp final, Luskins showed up, and Liana remembered their smell."

Elaine frowned. "What does that mean?"

No... no. This couldn't be true.

"It means if my father was behind Liana's kidnapping to keep us from bonding... then he somehow hired Luskins."

She frowned. "No. That's not possible. He hated Luska."

I nodded, and then everything got really quiet. For the first time since hearing Kohen's wild lies about my father, I became really afraid. Terrified that he might actually be telling the truth.

I was no longer tired; I was wide awake and going through every conversation I'd ever had with my father, every glare he'd ever given me, every correction to my behavior.

"Elaine?" She was leaning against the window, and I wasn't sure if she was asleep or not, but when she turned to face me, I saw that she was near tears.

Did she feel guilty for not telling me that sooner? Was she also replaying everything my father ever did or said to me to see if he was capable of murdering me?

"When you had the movers clean out my father's office, did you keep his things?"

She nodded. "In a secure storage unit, under guard. He had high-profile paperwork."

"Have everything brought to my office at the house. I want to go over it all."

I hated that I was doing this—that I had to. No one wanted to suspect their own father of hurting them. I felt sick to my stomach even thinking about it. He was strict, harsh even, but he would never plot to kill me.

Right?

I expected Liana to burst her way into my head then and tell me how she was glad I was finally looking into Kohen's claims about my father, but she was silent.

'I take no pleasure in your pain, young one,' she said then, and my heart fissured. I'd been so hard on her for the past two months, constantly at odds and fighting against her advice.

'I'm sorry. Kohen broke my ability to fully trust anymore,' I told her honestly.

'And he will have to answer for that. But he might also be right.'

I was not prepared for that. No way in any of the sixty days since Kohen admitted to killing my father and accusing him of a plot to kill me, did I think he could have been right.

I couldn't even comprehend it, so I sat back in the dark car and let the numbness seep in.

CHAPTER SEVEN

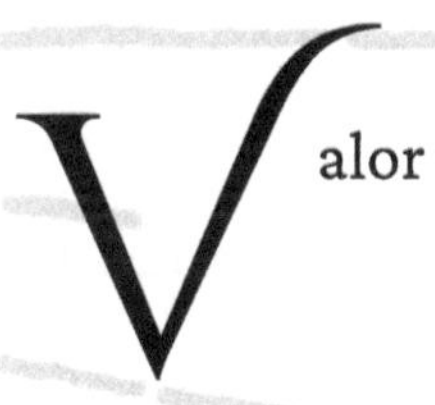

Valor

My watch beeped, and I pulled out another green flare. Tej reached out and stayed my hand. "I know you don't want your sister to worry about you, but you're telling her where we are going."

I frowned. "So?"

Tej pointed to the map. "If she figures out you're hunting Talanagi, she might come in and stop all of this."

"Did your brother tell you that?" I asked.

"No, but it's common sense. Your sister and my brother went where we're going. If you keep sending flares so far north, she might figure it out—not to mention Luska might notice."

With a groan, I stuck the green flare back into my pack. I was going out on a serious limb of trust here. "How do I know you're not just here to take out the empress' heir?" I asked Tej.

Arjun peered over his shoulder at me. "We could have done that by now. Besides, we're heirs too."

Technically, yes. I had heard that Kohen had officially been reinstated as king by his people. That would make them princes.

"I'm the heir. He's the spare." Tej elbowed Arjun, who scowled at him.

"Shut up!" he told his older brother.

Stars, they fought like cats and dogs, and they seemed so normal! If they were here to kill me, they were doing a poor job of it. They clearly weren't professional assassins. And why would Kohen send his heirs into harm's way? It didn't make sense.

A chuff to my right, I froze, the hairs on my neck standing straight up.

We all spun just as a gorgeous and deadly lioness padded out of the woods, eyes on me. Her fur was cream, and her ember marks glowed bright yellowish orange, like fire.

Tej quickly stepped in front of me, pulling his blade. "That's not who you bond," he declared.

I shoved him out of the way, locking eyes with the magnificent creature. There was so much intelligence in her gaze. "I may never have another chance for a strong bond. She's good enough," I said.

The lioness roared, and Arjun hooked his hand under my armpit and dragged me away. "Come on. Kohen said not to let you challenge anything other than the small red dragon."

I dug in my heels, but the bastard was strong, dragging me backward by the arm.

Tej was locked in a gaze with the lioness, speaking to her in low tones as if she could understand. Maybe she could.

"She was beautiful," I whimpered. It wasn't a Talanagi, but it was the next best thing.

"She's not for you," Arjun said as we followed the path around the corner and out of sight of the lion. She didn't pursue me. When a creature wanted to bond, they pursued you at all costs.

Maybe Arjun was right. If the bonding wasn't a good match—if she was too strong and dominant for me—I'd be dead. I relaxed in his grip, and he let go. But if I couldn't bond a lioness, or even pull my blade from a dead fox, how was I going to fight off a Talanagi?

Arjun must have picked up on my thoughts. "The bonding is taught in a scientific way in Amersea, but in Imbria, it's more spiritual. Their soul chooses yours, and it really isn't about physical strength. It's about spiritual strength. Your creature will see your soul, and the one you bond will choose you based on your spiritual strength."

"That's beautiful," I told him honestly.

He shrugged. "That's the way it is." He peered over his

shoulder, casting worried glances down the path, and I stopped walking.

"Okay, I won't bond her. Let's go back and make sure Tej is alright," I told him. I could see he was worried for his brother.

But right as I said it, Tej turned the corner. I scanned his face, from his hands down his body to his feet, but not a hair was out of place. No blood or wounds, either.

"What happened?" I asked.

"I convinced her to move on." He shrugged. "I didn't want to kill her, but I would if she didn't leave us alone."

My eyebrows rose. "You what?"

"Tej is an animal whisperer." Arjun nodded. "Always talking to the monkeys back home." Arjun made monkey noises and began to dance around his big brother, imitating a monkey. I laughed, and Tej rolled his eyes and pushed his brother off to the side, sending Arjun laughing.

Before I knew it, we'd walked three more hours north, my movements sluggish as I fought fatigue. The sun was just rising. We had officially made it through our first night.

My watch beeped, and I heard a hawk shriek above. I cocked my head just as a dark brown bird dive-bombed downward.

"Turn that thing off!" Tej snapped at my watch, pulling his blade as Arjun did the same, holding it up to the hawk that was barreling down at us.

When it got within ten feet of us, I relaxed. "Iniki!" I screamed, holding out my arm. She landed on my outstretched arm and peered from Tej to Arjun as if determining if I were safe.

"It's okay, they are with me," I told her, knowing that my sister must have worried when I didn't send the flares for the past few hours, and sent Iniki looking for me. Aisling was going to be pissed when she learned I was not sending them on purpose. Having Iniki check on me was illegal. If the admirals found out, they might say my sister tried to help me, and it would be bad.

Again, Iniki peered at Tej and Arjun, her beady eyes searing into them.

"Whose creature is that?" Tej asked.

"My sister's fiancé," I told them. I liked Alek. He was kind and loyal to the empire.

Tej and Arjun's eyes both bugged out of their heads. "Your sister is engaged?"

I nodded.

Iniki bent down and nipped at my finger, then looked at the boys again.

"They were waiting for me when I got here. They won't hurt me," I told her. "We are going to stick together and all bond creatures."

She squawked as if she hated that idea. Alek was no doubt relaying all of this to my sister, who was probably furious.

Iniki squinted at me with an angry glare, and I returned it. "Should you even be here? What if the admirals find out? I don't want the people of Amersea to think I got help. Tell my sister I'm fine and I won't be doing flares anymore. They are attracting creatures," I lied. "I was almost attacked."

Iniki cocked her head and peered back at the boys.

Tej held up his hands. "We are here to help."

Iniki squawked at him, launching off my hand and opening her wings wide so that Tej and Arjun fell backward, afraid. Then she took to the sky, screeching loudly.

Okay, that was... embarrassing.

I gave a nervous laugh. "My sister is protective."

Tej glanced up at the sky in annoyance. "Yeah, you can say that again."

I took off my watch, pressed the buttons to cancel my hourly alarm, and placed it in my pack. I was going all-in on this.

"You better not be lying to me about bonding a Talanagi," I told them.

Tej nodded. "Relax. Our brother knows what he's doing."

I couldn't believe I was following two Badshahs into Luksa. My sister was going to kill me.

CHAPTER EIGHT

A isling

"WHAT!" I shrieked as the sun poked over the horizon. Alek stood before me, having been woken from his bed, and rushed down here at my request after Valor missed her third flare. We agreed Liana was too big and would be spotted by guards—word would get back to the admirals that I'd given Valor help. But Iniki was small and could maybe spot Valor and see what was going on.

Alek stood before me, hair ruffled from sleep, eyes closed as he concentrated on seeing through Iniki's eyes. "She's with two Imbrians," he said again.

I panicked. "Who? How old are they? Is it Kohen? Anika? Do they have her tied up?"

Alek shook his head. "They're kids. Both boys. One is maybe fifteen-sixteen, the other a few years older. They seem friendly. She's saying they are together. Going to find creatures together. As a group."

I swayed on my feet so much that Elaine had to reach out and steady me.

Two boys. That age...

Kohen's brothers? *What the hell?* Like, what in the actual hell was going on?

"They are far north, near the Luskin border," Alek said, and I shared a look with Elaine.

"No," I whimpered. They wouldn't. Kohen wouldn't.

If he told my sister where to find Talanagi, I would rip his head from his body. I began to pace the gravel road. "That bastard!" Just when I thought Kohen might be right, and I had possibly made a mistake in my assessment of him, he did this.

"He's putting her in danger. To get her killed. It will look like an accident," I told Elaine.

She was frozen in thought as Vespa walked in circles around us.

'Come here,' Liana called to me, snapping me out of my tirade.

I walked over to her, distraught with worry, as I grasped her face and nuzzled into her neck feathers. It had been so long since I'd hugged her like this. Over the past two months, I'd grown further away from her. Something I deeply regretted at this moment.

'Do you want me to open my bond to Onyx?' she asked. She'd closed down her bond when they both betrayed us that night in the Wilds two months ago. We'd agreed it would stay closed.

'I don't want to hear Kohen's lies secondhand,' I told her.

She nodded, moving her head against me. *'But if he has a plan... if he's sending his brothers with Valor into Luska, we need to know.'*

My gut twisted at the thought of Valor in Luska.

'He wouldn't,' I whimpered, praying it wasn't true.

'He might if he had a vision and saw them successful. He might.'

If Kohen saw a vision about my sister, then I wanted to know what it was. But how could I believe anything that came from his mouth after he watched me grieve my own father and look for the killer for weeks, knowing he'd done it?

'I don't know. I feel frozen, incapable of making a decision,' I told her.

Liana nodded. *'Then let me decide for you. I will open my bond to Onyx, ask a few quick questions, and then close it. We can decide whether or not the information is false once we have it and what we want to do with it.'*

'Fine,' I croaked, pulling away from her and peering over to see Alek and Elaine speaking in hushed tones off to the side, where we had erected our tent.

No more than a minute passed, and I felt Liana bristle.

'Onyx confirms those are Kohen's brothers. He claims to have sent them to protect Valor. That she will bond a Talanagi. They are headed to Luska now.'

'No. It's a trap,' I told her, feeling a surge of panic as I envisioned my little sister taken and tortured by Maxim.

'Kohen claims both of his brothers and Valor will all bond Talanagi if they work together.'

'I don't want her to bond a Talanagi!' I snapped. *'I want her to stay in our territory!'*

She nodded. *'Before I closed the bond again, Onyx said that if you interfere and keep Valor from this, she will bond a lesser creature, and Amersea will not accept it. That it will be the end of the empire.'*

I let those words settle into me and wondered how I would feel if my great-great-grandfather's legacy were to end with me. I'd always been a bit uncomfortable with the fact that I was given an entire country simply because of birthright. But I'd seen what greed could do, what crooked politicians in high places could do. I would never be like that. Valor wouldn't either. We would keep Amersea safe. Prosperous.

I hated that right now I was being asked to trust the last person I wanted to. I should have killed him when I had the chance because now I was falling under Kohen's spell again. Inch by inch, he'd wormed his way into my heart, and now I was just confused.

'Tell Onyx that if my little sister dies or is gravely injured going after a Talanagi on Kohen's advice, I will fly into Imbria this very night and kill him.' I wasn't playing around anymore.

I'd been protecting Arjun and Tej from the war by not hitting the city of Sorak, but if they allowed Valor to perish, all bets were off.

Liana was silent a moment. *'He said if Valor sustains a mortal injury, he will submit himself to you, surrendering to your justice immediately.'*

I scoffed. What a perfect thing to say. I guessed now all we could do was wait.

And pray. I decided right then and there to start taking prayer more seriously.

May the stars watch over my little sister now.

CHAPTER NINE

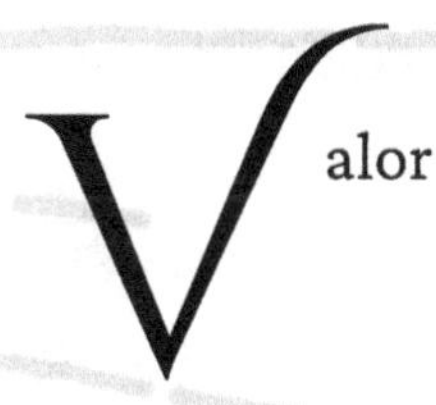

Valor

I COULDN'T BELIEVE my sister sent Iniki to look for me! Well, I could, but I was mortified. And scared of what her reaction would be. She now knew I was with Kohen's brothers. She was probably livid, ready to march in here and call the whole thing off.

"I wonder if my brother knows your sister is engaged?" Arjun asked.

"Who cares," I said.

Tej and Arjun shared a look.

"What?" I said when they didn't respond.

"When Kohen returned, and Aisling started bombing us, the people were ready to march on Amersea and take her head. We have more citizens than you do—ten to one."

That was a chilling calculation.

"We have better weapons, and more trained soldiers with bonded than you," I shot back.

Tej nodded as if agreeing. "But if one million people march across your border, eventually you'd get overrun."

My heart fluttered in my chest. Was that a threat?

"Calm down, little heir," Tej teased me. "I'm just telling you the facts because they were ready to kill your sister for bringing war to our lands after we just found peace."

"Well, why didn't they?" I asked as we walked deeper north. I could see the Wall now.

"My brother. He told everyone how he killed the emperor and that Aisling had every right to retaliate. He told them she was a woman of good character and would never harm a life without just cause. He spoke so passionately about her, people started to wonder if they had... been a couple."

I didn't know what to say to that, so I kept quiet. My mind couldn't deal with any of that right now.

After stopping to eat a meal and make more coffee, which we all shared, we trudged on throughout the day until we reached the Wall.

The boys stopped and consulted their map, and I felt nervousness eat at my stomach. I'd lost track of time. It was definitely day two. But how far into it, I didn't know. I pulled my watch out of my pack and balked at the time. It was dinnertime on the second day. We'd been walking forever with little rest. I felt so weary. There was no way I was going to be able to fight a Talanagi in this shape. I was dead on my feet, my eyelids heavy as well as my limbs. The coffee only made me jittery and didn't seem to give me any real energy.

Tej peered over at me, frowning. "You need rest," he commanded.

"No, I don't," I snapped, widening my eyes to look more alert.

He glanced at Arjun, who had dark circles under his eyes.

"You both do," Tej said. "We'll camp here for a bit. You sleep for four hours, we have a light meal, then we head over about midnight. Just as Kohen instructed."

"I'm not sleeping in the Wilds," I declared.

Tej glared at me. "I'll keep watch over both of you. I'm older. I don't need as much sleep as your young, growing minds," he taunted. Both Arjun and I launched at him. I punched his arm while Arjun went for his chest.

Tej laughed, rolling away from us. "Seriously though, get some sleep," he ordered.

I peered at Arjun, who yawned. "I don't feel like I can slay any dragons right now," he admitted.

"Me neither," I said. "But my sister told me not to sleep."

"Because you were alone. I will look out for you both. I promise." Tej placed prayer-clasped hands up to his chest and bowed deeply for dramatics.

I rolled my eyes. "Fine, but remember, my sister knows I'm with you now, so if you hurt me in any way—"

"Yeah, yeah." Tej waved me off. "Go to bed, kid."

I growled. He was incorrigible!

Arjun smiled a little at my bickering with Tej and rolled out his sleeping bag, pulling his blade out to hold it over his chest. He was ready to wake up and fight if needed.

I did the same, grasping the dagger they had given me, holding it as I slipped into my bag. I glanced over at Tej to see him sitting on a large flat rock, scanning the trees and then the sky, looking for any kind of threat.

It was crazy that just two days ago, I'd been mortal enemies with these guys, and now I was trusting one of them with my life while I slept. My sister would kill me if she knew, but I really hadn't trained well for the sleep deprivation, and it was hitting me hard. So hard, in fact, that the second I closed my eyes, I felt like I was melting into the earth. Then I was out.

A SMALL SHAKE on my shoulder had my eyes snapping open. I instinctively pulled my blade between me and the person hovering over me. Tej sneered down at me. "Not a morning person?" he asked as he stepped away from me.

It took me a second to figure out where I was and what was going on, but then everything came rushing back to me.

I peered up at the fire sky, trying to tell time based on the moon beyond it.

"It's near midnight," Tej told me.

I felt much better, less groggy, and more alert. I peered over to see Arjun yawning as he rolled up his pack.

"Thanks," I muttered to Tej, who had clearly kept watch the entire time. He looked tired.

"You want to rest?" I asked him.

He shook his head. "I'll be fine," was all he said. "But if you have any more coffee, I'll take that."

I handed him my satchel of ground coffee and then packed up my sleeping bag, shoving it into my pack. After we'd eaten a small amount of food, and Tej drank coffee while Arjun and I opted for water, we headed out.

Twenty minutes later, I couldn't believe I was doing this. As Tej lowered himself into the rushing river, bypassing the Wall and wading into Luska, I had a moment of panic.

Now was the time to turn back and try to bond that lioness. This was crazy. This would be how I died. My heart fluttered in my chest, but Arjun's words came back to me then.

"Because on the night of the second day, you bond a red dragon and fly yourself home. Safe. Alive. Powerful."

And then I thought of Kohen's letter.

If you do not bond a Talanagi, your people will say you are too young and weak to lead. They will revolt, and the empire will fall.

"Stars help me," I breathed, and then leaped into the frigid water. I was so short that the water came up to my chest, and I panicked as it began to tug me downstream. I knew how to swim, but I wasn't prepared to be floating alongside Luska for too long. I'd be spotted.

A strong hand grasped my arm and hauled me to the side. I peered over, expecting Tej, but it was Arjun. His face was fierce and determined as he struggled to pull me against the current, until we were close enough to the shore that Tej could pull us up out of the deep water.

"Thanks," I muttered to Arjun. I shuddered to think what would have happened had he not grabbed me so quickly. Just a few klicks down, there was a checkpoint. I knew the Luskins watched their waterways closely since they drank from this river and watered their crops with it. I'd heard my sister talking about it once.

I stepped onto the shore in soggy, water-logged boots and scowled. This was not very comfortable fighting attire.

Tej, who was much taller than me, and therefore only went to his waist, just shrugged as he looked down at me. "You'll have to make do."

"Okay, Dad," I retorted.

"Gross," Tej responded, which caused Arjun and me to share a smile. After squeezing as much water from the end of my shirt as possible. I pulled my blade, scanning the Luskin Wilds. I'd obviously never been to Luska, but I was very aware that if someone captured us and found out who I was, I'd be used as a pawn against my sister.

I reached down and smooshed my wet fingers into the dirt, then rubbed my cheeks with it until there were brown streaks across it. "If we get caught, my name is Natasia. We ran away from home, hoping to bond creatures for fun."

They both looked back at me like I was crazy.

"Hello, I'm the heir to Amersea. If I get caught—"

"Fine. I'm Zack. I'm an heir, too," Tej taunted.

"I'm Beast," Arjun said, and both Tej and I burst into laughter.

"Bro, I am *not* calling you that," Tej informed him as we began to walk deeper into the forest.

"You have to. I'm Beast, named after my incredible fighting skills." Arjun informed us of his fake backstory.

I couldn't stop smiling, even given the dire circumstances. Tej and Arjun, or Zack and Beast, had grown on me. I had wondered since hearing that my sister had some love affair with Kohen Badshah exactly how that had happened, but now I knew. It was little by little.

"So... who bonds first?" I whispered. "And what kind of Talanagi do you guys bond?" I was fully giving in to Kohen's vision, hoping it was real.

"Kohen didn't say," Tej told me. "He said it wasn't important. Just that you would bond a small red dragon. And we both would bond Talanagi as well."

I thought of my dagger still sticking out of the fox that had tried to kill Tej. I was so weak for not being able to pull it out. I felt stupid for it. I wanted to go back now and yank it out just to prove I could. Then maybe I'd show myself that I was ready to bond a Talanagi.

Tej stopped suddenly, and we all froze. He crouched down and picked up something bright blue, rubbing it between his fingers.

His eyes widened a little, not really in alarm—more in awe.

"What is it?" I whispered, stepping closer to inspect the blue... rock?

When he opened his palm, I gasped a little.

It wasn't a rock. It was a scale. A shimmery... dragon scale?

"Cool," Arjun said in low tones, stepping up beside me.

Excitement thrummed through me. Maybe this was all legit, Kohen's seeing the future, the map, everything.

I opened my mouth to speak when a blur of blue shot through the air and knocked Arjun to the ground. I spun, coming face to face with a blue dragon.

Holy crap.

It was huge.

I mean, at least to my five-foot-two height.

"She drew blood. You have to fight," Tej told his brother.

Arjun scrambled to get up, a small cut on his face.

I backed up, pulling my blade but slinking behind Arjun. Once blood was drawn, you couldn't interfere.

A twig snapped behind me and I spun that way, my heart leaping into my throat as a small red dragon stepped out of the thick trees.

No way.

"Uh... guys?" Tej called.

I risked a glance behind me to see a green dragon approaching him.

We were being attacked all at once. This was *so* not ideal!

Arjun suddenly gave a battle cry next to me and ran at the blue dragon, sinking his knife into her shoulder and using it as a handhold to mount her. She screeched, yanking away from him and bucking him off, sending him flying.

Tej was at my back then, pressing against me as we both

stepped in a slow circle, back to back. The green and red dragons moved around us like circling predators.

"This isn't normal. All at once like this," I told him. I'd never heard of multiple creatures hanging in a pack like this and trying to bond or attack at once.

"They're sisters," Tej whispered.

What?

"How do you know?" I breathed back.

"I just do." He seemed confused.

'Sister of the empress, eldest of three, I see you,' the creature before me spoke into my mind, and it terrified me. We hadn't even bonded yet. Could she do that?

I held my weapon aloft, gripping it as Tej grunted and buckled behind me, clearly struggling.

"Tej!" I shouted but didn't take my eyes off the beautiful creature before me.

'I've killed many larger than you,' the red dragon taunted as she moved to my left. She was smaller for a dragon but still larger than me. She stood maybe seven feet tall.

I thought about what Arjun had said, about the bonding not being all about physical strength.

'Maybe what I lack in size, I make up for in other areas,' I jested back, hoping she heard me.

Her eyes crinkled as if she were amused, and then, out of nowhere, she shot forward, opening her mouth to take my head!

Rolling to the side and out of the way, I popped up, dagger in my fist, and spun around just as she came back for another strike. I noticed at this distance that there were quite a few scars on her shoulder, maybe where previous Lottery winners had tried to bond her. I wasn't even sure if Luska did a lottery or—

"Valor!" Tej yelled in warning as the red dragon's tail whacked me in the side of the head. I was flung to the ground, landing hard on my elbow as pain throbbed inside my head. Blackness danced at the edge of my vision as a high-pitched ringing whined in my ears. Copper tang filled my mouth, and I spat on the mossy earth.

Blood.

The bonding had begun.

This was it.

My gaze flicked quickly to Tej, who was battling the green dragon. Arjun was on the back of the blue dragon, trying to choke it into submission.

The red dragon just stood there, peering down at me with curiosity.

'I thought I felt a strong power in you. I guess not,' she said as I stayed down, curled on my side.

"Please don't hurt me," I whimpered, putting as much patheticness as I could into my voice. Aisling always told me I was too dramatic and would make a good stage actress. Now was the time to test my skills.

The red dragon snarled down at me, seemingly disgusted with my weakness. My whole life I'd been second place—second to Aisling, too small, too young, too immature, never good enough. I realized now that it had built a well of rage inside of me. I had a deep desire to prove myself to everyone: Elaine, my little sisters, Aisling, my country, this dragon. She was looking at me like I was a pile of excrement.

I held out my hand to her, sobbing. "Please, just let me go."

Her nostrils smoked, and I watched her like any prey watched a predator. The second I saw her muscles twitch, I burst from my position just as she lunged for me, mouth open, and we collided in the air.

I drove my dagger into her open mouth, pinning her tongue to the bottom of her jaw like it had been pierced.

She roared in anger as smoke billowed out of her so thickly I couldn't see my hand in front of me. Trying to remember where she was, I leaped forward, grasping out blindly, and felt her cold scales. Digging my fingers into them, I climbed onto her back and bent down into her ear.

"Don't *ever* underestimate me," I growled, and colors exploded out of her, filtering through the smoke and throwing rainbows all over the forest. The lasers sliced through the swirling smoke like threads of molten color, each beam igniting the haze, and I heard a whoop of excitement that I thought was Arjun.

I felt it then. What they told us about in books, but Aisling said could never truly be described—a squeeze in my heart so tight I thought it might burst. *The bond.* Then, all at once, I was imprinted with information about her. She was one of three sisters, but they weren't triplets. She was the youngest. She and her sisters longed to leave the Wilds but had never found anyone worthy and didn't want to break up and leave each other. She instantly knew everything about me as well. That I was Aisling's heir to the empire, never feeling good enough or strong enough, but that I had a strong desire to prove myself.

Reaching down, I pulled the dagger from her mouth.

'Thank you,' she said. I hoped she had self-healing powers because that had to hurt.

The smoke cleared, and when I peered over, a grin pulled at my lips.

Arjun and Tej were both mounted on the other dragons. They were slightly bloodied, but nothing life-threatening.

'My eldest sister, Elvria, the green dragon, is the wise and quiet one of us.' She nodded to Elvria. *'Siara is the lively comedic relief.'* She then flicked her head to the dragon Arjun was riding.

She already knew I was a triplet, and that I was the younger sister of Aisling. *'What does that make you?'* I asked her.

'The sassy, rebellious one,' she snickered.

Elvria stiffened, cocking her head to the side. *'We must go now. I smell humans.'* I heard her rich, husky tones in my head, and my eyes widened.

'We can mentally communicate with anyone, bonded or not. It's a power we all share,' Zara told me.

Wow, that was incredible.

'Hold on,' she added, and I leaned forward, wrapping my arms around her neck.

I peered at Tej, who also clung to his dragon, looking slightly nervous, and then at Arjun, who looked absolutely green in the face and ready to vomit. Then Zara kicked off the ground, and I was pinned to her back with the inertia.

"Weeee!" Tej screamed.

"I'm gonna puke!" Arjun called out.

I just laughed. I'd always wanted to fly, and never in a million years did I think I'd have the chance. I had hoped to one day beg Liana to take me for a ride, but now I wouldn't have to.

We hit the top of the tree canopy and I could see the Wall beyond, about a hundred yards away.

There was a freeness to flying, the cold wind through my hair. My clothes were still damp, so I was actually freezing at this speed, but I didn't care! It was the greatest—

I suddenly couldn't breathe, like the air had been pulled from my lungs. In a panic, I peered behind me to see a blond female rider on a large red dragon. The red rider. My sister had told me about her.

She was grinning ear to ear as I struggled to breathe, and from the look on Tej's and Arjun's faces, they were feeling the same.

'I can't breathe!' I told Zara.

She dive-bombed, and I slid forward two feet, nearly falling off her. All three dragon sisters split up then, flying in different directions. When Zara had put some distance between us and the red rider, oxygen came back to my lungs, and I gasped for air.

'That's Oryana and her bonded. She's our mother.'

Oh great.

Her mother was chasing us and trying to kill me!

'What do we do?' I asked as she flew closer to the wall, the red rider right on our tail.

'Do you feel any powers emerging yet?' Zara asked me.

I didn't. I was way too panicked.

Reaching into my pack with a shaky hand, I pulled the handful of flares I had left. When I saw the red one, I ripped off the cap and pressed the button, shooting a red firework into the sky. Then I couldn't breathe again, as the red rider was right on top of me once more.

CHAPTER
TEN

isling

I FELT HALF dead on my feet, so tired I could sleep for a week, but at the same time, I was alert, fueled by anxiety for my sister.

She was probably in the Luskin Wilds right now. It was nearly midnight and no flares, no contact. We'd driven by car even farther north, just outside Sky Reach, nearly at the Wall. If she was going into Luska, I wanted to be close in case she needed me.

"Alek, can you send Iniki to go look for her again?" I begged him. He was right by my side, getting me coffee and telling me Valor was strong and would be okay. I'd pulled him out of bed after Valor stopped sending flares, and he'd never complained.

Iniki peered at Alek, then at the two guards who stood at the fence line.

"I will if you want, but it might seem like preferential treatment." Alek offered.

I glared at the guards, reporting back everything to the admirals so they could say Valor had no help. I wanted to throttle them right now and go check on my sister.

"No, you're right. Let's wait a bit," I agreed.

Liana came up behind me then, nuzzling my side with her head. *'Want to go for a fly over Sky Reach? Take your mind off of things? You may not see her until morning. It's a far walk that deep north.'*

I heard what Liana said, but I also sensed something else behind her words. Like maybe if we were high in the sky, I might be able to peek over into the Wilds and see Valor?

"No harm in a night ride," I told her.

I walked over to the guards. "I'm going for a flight over Sky Reach. Report to me immediately if you have any word on my sister."

They nodded.

Elaine assured me she would also keep watch and be here for Valor if she got out.

"Mind if Iniki joins you?" Alek asked.

Having Alek here and being able to depend on him in my time of need spoke volumes about the person he was.

"I'd like that," I told him, and Iniki leaped for the skies. I knew she could report back to him anything I wanted.

I slid onto Liana's back, resting in the saddle, and then we were off.

The second we hit above the trees, I craned my neck for any sign of my sister. The trees in the Wilds were so thick, coupled with the glow of the fire sky—like a burning vein down the countryside—it made it hard to see anything.

Iniki soared alongside us as Liana made slow circles around the base. I peered at the Wall, and it felt so weird to see only two men patrolling it. Normally, it was packed with our soldiers. But since the Luska front had died down, we'd put our resources into other things.

I was just about to look back over at the Wilds when a shot of red caught my attention. A flare shot up into the sky.

Red flare. *Valor*.

Without even asking, Liana shot through the sky in that direction.

My heart raced as I thought of all the different scenarios. Valor's flare had come from the *other* side of the wall, in Luska. She was captured. I knew it.

We flew faster than normal, sailed over the Wall, and then shot downward. Instantly, I saw a scene that my brain could barely comprehend.

There were four figures scattered in the air, all riders on dragons. When I looked closer, I saw two of them were Arjun and Tej, Kohan's little brothers. And I gasped when I noticed my little sister riding a small red dragon.

'She bonded a Talanagi,' I said with absolute pride, but it quickly quenched when I noticed she was clawing at her throat, lips purple.

I found the fourth rider, and my blood boiled.

"Stop!" I shouted at the red rider, throwing out my power. Her gaze flew towards me, wide-eyed, and I knew she was remembering the last time we met when I'd likely broken both of her legs by making her jump from her dragon. Not something I was proud of.

The silvery cord shot out of me and wrapped around her, and then I heard my sister gasping for air beside me. The red rider yanked her dragon's neck and fled the scene, no doubt wanting to avoid my forcing her to jump again. I wanted to go after her, to kill her so she couldn't be a problem anymore, especially now that I knew she was Maxim's twin sister.

But I needed to get Valor and Kohen's little brothers out of here before she got backup. We were still at war with her people, just taking a suspiciously long break that I wasn't questioning.

I peered at Valor, wondering if she'd put two and two together that I'd just made her stop or if it had looked like I'd just arrived and she'd fled in fear.

"Can we get out of here?" Valor asked me, peering anxiously over her shoulder.

I nodded, then looked to Arjun and Tej.

"Follow me!" I told them all, my mind spinning with the fact that they *all* rode dragons!

I couldn't land us at Sky Reach, not with two Badshahs! Kohen's little brothers would be taken into custody, and I didn't want to explain why I hadn't arrested them yet. They were the perfect pawns to lure Kohen to me. If I threw them in the brig, then sent word to Kohen that I would set them free if he surrendered himself, he would come. I knew he would. And yet... I couldn't do that. I wanted justice for my father's murder, but not at the hand of kidnapping children.

I flew over the base, and Iniki was suddenly there in the sky. "Tell our men these people are with me and not to blow the horn," I told her.

She zoomed downward to the base and over to the guard tower, which watched the skies. Three dragons and a firebird flying over Amersea was a sight to behold, something my people were not used to. They had barely just gotten used to me—and Colt bonded to his griffin. Valor's dragon bonding was good, very good for our people, but it would take time for them to know not to shoot her down.

I peered over at my sister. Her face was covered in mud, she was shivering from cold, and she looked like hell, but she was grinning. The wind whipped her short hair around her face as she stroked her dragon. I shook my head.

"Are you hurt?" I screamed over the wind. "Need medical?"

She looked at me and shook her head.

"I'm proud of you!" I told her, and she smiled wider.

"Thanks!"

"Go and present yourself to Elaine and the two guards at the northern gate to the Wilds. They will report to the admirals that you have legally bonded a Talanagi."

She nodded and peered over at Arjun and Tej.

"Thank you," she told them.

Both boys nodded to her. *Thank you?* Did they help her? *Of course, they did.* They'd been in there two days together.

"Follow me!" I told the boys and veered left over the Wilds, just below the fire sky. The moment we entered the dome of protection, the small pieces of ember fell around us, and I tried not to be taken with how beautiful it was.

I lowered Liana to the ground in an open clearing, and the boys followed.

'What are you doing, Aisling?' Liana asked.

'I have no idea,' I told her honestly.

They had Talanagi now, who I could tell from one look were very powerful. Maybe not as powerful as Liana, but together, I wouldn't doubt they were going to be powerful men in Kohen's army one day.

I stepped off of Liana and looked up at the boys, who slid down off their green and blue dragons.

"Why did you help my sister?" I asked them.

"Kohen told us to," Tej said.

"Why? So that you could ask her things? Ferret out our secrets? Gain her trust?"

Tej glared at me, and Arjun looked hurt.

"You're stupid, you know that?" Arjun said bluntly.

"Excuse me?"

"Yes. You heard me. You're constantly thinking the worst of us, and all we were trying to do was protect Valor."

"Which makes me stupid?" I asked. "We're at war, Arjun! The enemy doesn't just send over his brothers and crown princes to look after my sister. That's not *normal* enemy behavior. What's the catch?"

"You're right." Tej stepped closer to me, and my heart pinched—he looked so much like Kohen. "The enemy doesn't send his heirs into enemy territory normally. That's because Kohen isn't your enemy, Aisling. You've been barking up the wrong tree this whole time."

"He killed my father!"

"Who was trying to kill you!" Tej roared back at me. "My brother told me everything. You're empress now. You could open a full investigation over who tried to kill you in boot camp, who attacked the train. Why haven't you?"

Shock ripped through me at that assessment. I *was* empress now. I could command anything. Didn't I want to know who was in charge of the attempt on my life? Who tried to kill us all by derailing the train and sending those Luskins to attack?

Deep down inside of me, among the darkest part of myself, I heard the answer.

No. I didn't want to know. I was scared of the truth. I was scared it *was* my very own father.

My bottom lip shook, and Tej backed down, stepping away from me.

"My brother tells everyone you will be our future queen, that you will be our future sister-in-law." Tej looked disgusted with me. "Stop bombing us and find out the truth for yourself."

Kohen shouldn't be telling people that.

"Have you ever thought that maybe your brother lies to you?" I snapped.

Tej leveled his gaze at me. "Ever thought your father lied to you?"

That one sentence ripped me open inside, and without

another word, they got on their dragons and left, heading for Imbria.

The dam I had built around my emotions, around my sanity, fissured then. The harsh words of a seventeen-year-old boy had broken me. Tears leaked from my eyes, and a numb pain spread throughout my chest. I sank to my knees.

Liana walked closer to me until her head was nuzzled into my neck. A sob built in my throat. Emotional agony I hadn't thought possible to hurt so much tore through my chest.

I grabbed my arms and rocked back and forth. Kohen, my father, Kohen, my father. Who to believe, who to trust? One of them was gaslighting me. I felt my mind fraying at the edges, as I feared losing myself to darkness.

'Shhh, stay with me, young one. We will figure this out together,' Liana told me.

'What if Kohen was right, and I've lit half of his country on fire in anger?'

'He killed your father and lied about it. Even if he was protecting you, he should have handled it differently. Call a cease-fire for a week. Let's do an investigation and find the truth.'

It was good advice. *'What if he was wrong? What if Kohen has been playing a game with me this entire time?'*

Liana stood to her full height. *'Then no more messing around. We send a letter to Kohen saying we believe him and want to meet him, then we gut him open like a fish.'*

Considering he was impervious to my power, that was about our only option. I nodded and then wiped my eyes, sliding onto her back as we took to the skies. As I peered over my shoulder, I saw that most of Imbria was burning, and guilt sank into my stomach like a stone.

CHAPTER ELEVEN

Aisling

I ASKED Elaine to tell Commander Ledger that we were entering into a one-week ceasefire with Imbria and to draft up an agreement and send it to Kohen to sign. Then I told her to get some sleep, as I was about to do. After about five hours of rack time, I showered quickly and met the admirals in the war room at Sky Reach for a meeting. The second I entered, the shouting began.

"What is with the ceasefire with Imbria!?" Commander Ledger demanded.

"We almost have them by the balls!" Admiral Caruso agreed.

Then, they all began shouting at once. I already had a headache.

"Quiet!" Elaine yelled, and everyone stopped speaking.

I sighed, knowing I couldn't very well tell him I wanted to investigate reports of my own father trying to harm me. "I would like the people of Amersea to enjoy this reprieve, take some time to relish in the news of my engagement, and—"

"Horseshit!" Commander Ledger shot. "You've wanted Badshah dead since day one of this war. Now it's two months in, and I'm about to serve you his head on a silver platter. If you—"

I reached out and grasped the sides of his jaw. "What did you just say to me?" I asked him.

His eyes widened so big I thought they might fall out of his head. He'd been disobedient and mocking for weeks now, and I was sick of it.

"Your job is to take my orders. You are temporarily relieved of duty, Commander. Go home for a week and enjoy your family."

I released his face, and he staggered backward, stunned.

"Admiral Caruso will be acting commander until Commander Ledger returns in one week," I told her and everyone else in the room.

She looked dumbfounded, but nodded.

Ledger went from shock to fury as he stormed from the room and slammed the door, his creature trailing behind him.

"Does anyone else have a problem following orders?" I asked.

"No, Empress," came the resolute reply.

I left the room, unhappy with how I'd handled things. I didn't want to be the leader who required blind loyalty, but too often, over the past two months, Ledger thought he controlled me and my decisions. He needed a slap on the hand.

Elaine stepped out of the war room, and I prepared myself for a lecture.

"Messenger got back a few hours ago while you were sleeping. Kohen signed the peace treaty. You have a week."

"Why didn't you tell me sooner?"

"You were too busy putting Commander Ledger on forced leave," she said with a smirk.

I sighed. "I'm going to head to Riverine. Check on the girls." I lowered my voice. "Did you have that stuff sent to the house from the storage unit?"

She nodded. "It should be there by the time you get there."

"Want to come?" I asked her, gesturing to Liana.

She shook her head. "I have a few more things to deal with here. I'll come check on you and the girls tomorrow?"

"Alright." I slung my leg over Liana and took to the skies. By the time we made it to the house in Riverine, I was starving. I'd forgotten to eat breakfast after having slept in.

"Aisling!" Victory rushed out onto the lawn when she saw Liana land. I grinned, waving to the guard posted at the door as Victory leaped into my arms. Liana walked over to the forest behind the house, where I saw Valor's new creature lying in the sun.

"Can you believe Val bonded a Talanagi? When can Virtue and I go? We want a dragon too!" Victory pouted.

I smiled at her. "When you're nineteen, like everyone else."

"No fair!" Virtue spat from the doorway. "Why should Valor get special treatment?"

Ugh, I didn't want to come home to a fight.

Victory seemed to sense that and spoke for me: "Because she's older, and Father is dead. Come on, let's show Ash the cupcakes we made with Tetra."

"Tetra's here!" I brightened, letting Vic lead me inside as I tried to forget how easily Victory had just stated that our father was dead.

When I stepped inside, I was hit with the earthy aroma of cinnamon, nutmeg, and... "Carrot cake!" I practically ran to the kitchen and plucked up a cupcake teeming with frosting.

"Hey." Tetra hobbled over and pulled me into a side hug while I shoved the muffin into my mouth.

"Hefy," I managed around the cupcake. Sweet goodness exploded on my tongue, and I glanced at Valor, who was staring intently at Tetra's crooked foot. Tetra wasn't wearing socks; her cane was leaning against the far kitchen wall. Her foot was an angry red, and she seemed to be having a bad pain day. I cleared my throat, and Valor peered up at me guiltily.

It wasn't like her to stare at Tetra's foot. They'd grown up seeing it, so there was nothing "abnormal" about it. She must just be tired, caught in a stare.

"Is Gwen here?" I asked.

"I gave her a couple of hours off to see her family in town," Tetra said, and I nodded.

"Did you sleep at all?" I asked Valor.

She nodded. "Barely." She'd showered and cleaned up, and I noticed she seemed more... sure of herself. She was confident, and that made me happy.

"I meant to ask your creature's name last night," I told her.

"Zara," Valor said, peering out the window at Zara and Liana through the backyard.

"It's weird at first, but you two will figure each other out. Likes and dislikes," I told her. "I tried to put Liana in the barn like a horse our first night."

Tetra and the triplets all burst into laughter. "Did she breathe fire on you?" Victory asked, grinning.

"No, she was gracious." But the moment I said it, I was reminded of that night when Liana asked me if I loved my father and told me she wouldn't tell me what she thought of him. It pulled at my mind now. I had forgotten.

I shook my head to clear my thoughts. "Have your powers shown up?" I casually asked Valor. Her gaze flicked to Tetra's foot for a split second, but she shook her head. "Maybe I should go to boot camp like you, and it will come out."

I laughed, and Tetra joined in.

"Nice try." Tetra ruffled her hair, and Valor batted her hand away.

"Why not?" Valor pouted.

"There is no cohort to train with, first of all," I told her. "And you're—"

She dared me to say "too young" with her glare.

"Too *valuable*. I'll have private trainers come."

"Fine," she growled. "There's a bunch of crap in your office. Elaine had some men move boxes in all morning, which is why I couldn't sleep."

"Sorry," I told her and then flicked my gaze to Tetra. "Want to meet me in my office?" I asked her, grabbing a second cupcake.

She nodded. "See you later, girls. Thanks for baking with me."

They gave her a hug, and she grabbed her cane, walking behind me as she dragged her foot. I glanced back at Valor to see her eyes trained on Tetra's bad foot. Something about it piqued my curiosity, but I had enough to worry about right now. I'd have to ask her about it later.

Once Tetra and I got into my office, Tetra whistled low at the boxes leaning high in the corner. There must have been about twenty-five of them. *Way* more than I thought.

"Hey, is your foot okay?" I asked her now that we were alone.

She waved me off. "Just a bad day. What's up with all this?" She gestured to the stack of boxes taking up half my office.

I sighed. "You're going to want to sit down," I told her.

She did, looking at me warily.

"After you left last night, Valor stopped sending green flares. I called Alek over, and Iniki went looking for her."

Tetra didn't seem too concerned by my story, especially since she'd just seen Valor alive and well in the kitchen.

"She was with Kohen's little brothers," I told her. I'd ordered Valor not to tell anyone she'd been with the Badshah brothers for now.

"What!" she screeched, sitting up straighter.

I then launched into everything, telling her about Kohen's note before my engagement party, which explained I could be happy with Alek, and then about what Onyx had said when Liana contacted him, and then again what his brothers had said as I saw them off in the Wilds.

When I was finished, Tetra squirmed in her seat as she peered at the boxes. "So all this is from your father's office?"

I nodded.

"And we need to find something to either incriminate your father, whom you loved, or Kohen, whom you loved."

I swallowed hard at her assessment, not realizing until now that either way this went, someone I loved had betrayed me.

"Yes." My voice shook.

Tetra stood, leaning on her cane as she stepped before me. "Are you sure this is what you want?"

I released a shaky breath. "I want the truth," I told her.

She frowned, as if that made her sad.

"I thought this was what you wanted? For me to investigate Kohen and Anika's claims about my father..."

"I do, Aisling. But I'm afraid they will be right, and I'm not sure I want to see the moment my best friend finds out her father tried to murder her." The room was heavy with her words like a thick fog had settled in.

On the one hand, it would kill me to find out that my entire life he'd trained me to be his successor, only to attempt to kill me because I grew stronger than him. But the alternative was worse: not knowing, continuing to punish Imbria and banish Kohen when he might really have been trying to protect me. The truth was, I wanted those kisses to be real, those I love yous and... all of it. I wanted what Kohen and I had to be real. And if it wasn't, if Kohen had been messing with me this whole time and implanted all of this in my head as some long game so he could get his country back, then stars help him, I'd burn the whole thing down.

"I need this," I told her.

Tetra nodded. Without saying another word, she walked over to a box, ripped the lid off, and grabbed a hunk of papers. "I'll start with this box. You start with that." She nudged a box closer to me, and I sat down and got to work.

There was probably top-secret security clearance stuff in here, and I didn't trust just anyone to go through it. Only Elaine and Tetra and myself would be in this office over the next several days.

WE SKIMMED papers for what seemed like forever, and didn't really find anything crazy. My father was hoarding some alcohol and high-value items for himself and wrote them off as being used for the Fleet, but other than that, he was squeaky clean. I was starting to get depressed that Kohen had been playing a game with me all along.

There was a knock at the door. "Dinner!" Victory yelled.

We emerged from the office and out into the dining room, where Gwen was back and just setting out a plate full of chicken drumsticks and honeyed cornbread.

"Yum. I'm starved," I said, and Gwen went stiff, saluting me.

"Empress."

I rolled my eyes. "Gwen, we talked about this. At home, we are at ease. You're not a sergeant, and I'm not an empress."

She looked confused.

"Okay, well, we still are those things, but just be at ease," I told her, and she relaxed her posture.

"Yes, Empress."

Good enough. I liked Gwen. She was strict with the girls but still loving. She was no Elaine, but as close as you could get. We'd let most of the staff go on paid leave for now, trying to limit knowledge of where my sisters lived. Gwen cooked, cleaned, did laundry, everything a mother would do, and I was grateful to her.

Tetra leaned her cane against the wall and hobbled over as my gaze flicked to Valor. She was starting at Tetra's foot again!

I kicked her under the table, and her head snapped up to me. Guilt marred her features, and she reached for a chicken drumstick.

What was going on with her?

"Look at Ariyel with the girls," Tetra said as she passed the window. We all peeked out to see her wolf lying in the grass with Zara and Liana. Even Gwen's owl creature was flying circles above them.

"I want a creature early, too!" Virtue argued. "It's not fair that only Valor gets one."

I sighed, tearing into a chicken drumstick. I was already sick of this argument. I was willing to bet it was going to repeat every week until they were nineteen. They would probably wear me down by their sixteenth birthday and I'd let them go early just to shut them up.

Parenting was exhausting.

I opened my mouth to tell Virtue to give it a rest when the sirens rang out. The war sirens, the new ones I had installed in case there was a repeat of what happened the night my father died.

An attack on Riverine.

I burst up from the table so fast my chair knocked over. Tetra limped to her cane, wincing with each pressure she put on her foot.

"What's happening?" Victory whimpered.

"Keep them safe," I told Gwen, who was already pulling a hidden katana out of a kitchen cupboard.

I was halfway out the door with Tetra on my heels when Valor ran up beside me. "I'm going too."

"No, you're not!" Gwen, Tetra, and I all said at once.

"I have a Talanagi!" she growled.

"With no battle training and *no* gift yet. Get inside and

stay alive!" I barked, physically pushing her back into Gwen, who pinned her to her chest.

I let the door slam behind me, ignoring Valor's screams, and ran for Liana.

'Is Kohen attacking after our truce? I'll kill him,' I told her.

'I just asked Onyx. He said it's not them,' she told me, already bent down so that I could leap on her back and into my saddle.

I stopped when Zara stood, and I met my sister's creature's gaze head-on. "Your job is to keep Valor safe. Until she's eighteen, you both live under *my* rules. You cannot join the fight today," I told her sternly.

Zara's voice in my mind was a surprise. *'I would never take her into battle so soon.'*

'Part of her magic,' Liana told me.

"Okay, well, thank you," I told her, not wasting any more time on that. When I spun to tell Tetra I'd fly over the city to try to see where the fighting was coming from, my heart sank. She was way behind me, whimpering in pain as she limped across the grass on her cane. Ariyel pounced across the space to meet her.

It was a bad pain day. I didn't want to force her, but her power had the incredible ability to save lives.

"If you can't—" I shouted to her, climbing on Liana's back.

"Go! I'll follow you," she told me, chucking her cane like it was cursed, and leaped on Ariyel's back, sitting up with confidence as Ariyel dashed across the yard and out front.

Whoa.

I tried not to think about the fact that Tetra was riding her wolf into a battle just like Kohen predicted.

Fine, he could see the future, that much I would admit, but it didn't mean everything he said he saw about the future was true. He could have lied. Liana flew up, and I didn't have time to even dwell on Kohen because the second we hit the sky, a scream tore from my lungs.

Emberlane Park was on fire, and over a dozen flying Talanagi creatures with Luskin riders hovered high above it. Rage boiled inside of me as I watched our Fleet soldiers trying to fight them from the ground. But they shot projectiles into the air, and the Talanagi riders flew out of the way, dodging them. We'd been taken by surprise. Again. Because we didn't have enough flying creatures.

'Kohen is coming with Onyx to help,' Liana told me as she flew closer to the fire, and I pulled my arrow.

'What? No! Why did you keep the bond open? I don't want his help.'

'I opened it briefly to ask if they were attacking and then forgot to close it. I'm sorry.'

'It's fine, but tell Onyx if Kohen comes, I'll kill him.' I knew the threat was empty the second I said it. I was so confused where Kohen was concerned.

He killed my father, I reminded myself.

'Can we take all of them?' I asked Liana, surveying the dozen or so flying Talanagi.

'Without you exposing your hidden power? We can try,' she said. *'They will know you can explode into fire from the last battle, so I'm guessing they will try to evade us and spread out.'*

What was their endgame? Burn all of Riverine? Send a message? There was only one way to find out.

Liana flew fast and hard towards the blaze and the enemy hovering above it. Out of my periphery, I spotted a blur of blue. My head whipped in that direction to see Colt barreling towards me.

"I was on leave in town. How can I help?" he shouted over the wind and now roaring fire below. We were only a couple hundred feet from the enemy.

Colt's power with his new creature was control over water. It was like the stars had sent him at the perfect time.

"Can you make it rain before they burn our entire capital down?" I asked him.

He nodded. "You got it." He reared back and out of harm's way. He was still working on his power and had to concentrate to focus it.

It was just me then.

As I approached, ten of the dozen flyers branched off and retreated, heading towards the cove to our west, causing confusion to rise up inside of me.

The two left were the red rider and a male on a green griffin with blue ember marks. They waited for me as if they wanted to talk or something.

'What's going on?' I asked Liana. The enemies who had retreated were still going, not just getting distance because they might have known about my ability to control minds. They were leaving. One of our men was able to shoot a harpoon and bring the rider of a fleeing creature down, but the rest got away.

"What the hell do you want!?" I shouted at the red rider female. The smoke and heat from the fire billowed behind me.

She grinned as if pleased with herself. "My brother wanted to send you a little message." She gestured to the burning park behind us.

"Oh yeah, what's that?" I asked.

"The Talanagi are ours!" she spat. "If you come on our land again and steal one, we will steal one of your sisters."

Threatening my sisters to my face was about the last thing any person should ever do. I couldn't let her live after that. My silence seemed to have sent her a message because I watched the moment fear crossed over her face, and she attempted to pull her dragon back.

'End her,' Liana agreed.

I'd been practicing with my power. Little things on Elaine, with her permission. I think I was ready to try now.

'Jump.' I pushed my power out to her mentally, like I would to Liana, without having to speak out loud. The silver cord flew from my lips and wrapped around her mind, and then I pushed a thought to her dragon.

'Freeze.' And a second cord flew from me and into the dragon.

Her eyes widened.

"No!" she screamed as she stood on her dragon, legs shaking.

"What are you doing!?" the man on the griffin beside her yelled.

'Jump!' I pushed. I could feel her fighting it. Then she

just walked off the edge of her dragon and leaped to her death. I watched her fall, the sickening thud of her body reaching me from all the way up here. Her dragon was rooted to the spot, unable to chase after her to save her, and the man with her was now screaming in shock. He looked at me wide-eyed.

"You're evil!" he spat, backing up as his griffin flew away from me.

"Tell Maxim if he threatens one of my sisters again, I'll kill him!" I roared.

I'd forgotten what happened when a bonded died outside the Wilds. The red rider's dragon gasped for air, plummeting to the ground, where her body lay at an odd angle just outside the burning park. Then it began to rain.

Something dark moved inside of me, like a beast asking to be fed, and I knew it was my power, the power to control others.

'Did I go too far?' I asked Liana, my voice of reason. She threatened my little sister! I had to stop that. But making her jump, forcing her against her will, it made me sick.

You're evil, that man had said. Was he right?

'I'm the wrong person to ask,' Liana said. *'My grandmother once made a male firebird drown himself because he tried to force his way on one of my daughters. Seemed perfectly reasonable to me.'*

I could feel the smile in her voice as she recounted the memory. I was shocked she spoke of the past. She rarely did, and it took my attention away from my own guilt.

'You had daughters before the Great Fall?' I asked her. I had

assumed all of her children were bred here with her mate and then perished.

'I do,' she said.

Do? Shock ripped through me. *Do*. Not *did*. If she had daughters, that meant they were immortal. That meant...

Sorrow bloomed to life in my chest as I thought of what it must be like to have been parted from your own children. I didn't know what the great fall was or much about her family, but I felt bad now that she was stuck here with me and away from them.

'You don't think I went too far?' I asked her again.

'Let me ask you something: if you could have pulled a knife across her throat to kill her that way, would you have?'

'Yes,' I answered immediately, as the rain fell harder and the fire smoked and sizzled below.

'You don't regret killing her, only how you did it.'

'Yes,' I agreed.

She nodded. *'My grandmother also had these feelings. And when the Fall happened, she was about to step down as Tsarina over it.'*

That was surprising. *'Because of her power?'* I asked.

'Sort of,' Liana said vaguely.

'Well, who would have ruled in her place? What power did they have?' I assumed it was her mother.

'Me. I think we should get out of this rain now,' she told me, and I recognized that this conversation was over.

For the first time since Liana had told me about this "Great Fall," I began to wonder more about what had happened, but I kept my mouth shut.

We flew to the ground, where Tetra and over fifty Fleet soldiers had amassed. They watched the burning park with apprehension. I didn't think anyone saw what I'd done to the red rider as she was on the other side of the blaze, out of view.

"They were just sending a message!" I barked out, scanning the faces of the men and women for people I knew. I spotted Charlene, happy to see her wearing a Fleet uniform. Commander Ledger pulled up in his car along the main road as the soldiers broke into questions.

"What message?"

"Are we going to send a message back?"

I weighed a lot of things in my head then. Being a leader, you had to make quick decisions, and that's what I was going to do.

"The Talanagi are all on the Luskin side of the wall!" I bellowed, and shocked gasps rang out through the soldiers and crowd present. Some people who lived at the edge of the park were walking over now that the fire was being put out by the rain.

"That's where I bonded Liana, and that's where my sister bonded her dragon yesterday," I admitted.

More shocked gasps, and I could tell by the look on Commander Ledger's face he didn't like what I was saying, but he kept quiet, especially since he was technically on leave from his duties.

"They think they own the Talanagi!" I bellowed. "So let's prove them wrong."

Roars of excitement ripped through the amassed Fleet soldiers.

"I'm calling for the east side of the Wall within the Wilds to be torn down! Then, we will have an emergency Lottery. All men and women ages eighteen to twenty-five can enter. Even if you have entered before and weren't chosen." I met Charlene's gaze.

The cheers and roars were deafening. People jumped up and down and hugged each other. Clearly, many here had not been chosen to bond in the past and were excited to do so now.

Commander Ledger walked over and met my gaze. "I think it's the best plan you've had since you took over," he admitted.

I grinned. "Are you only saying that so I'll end your leave early?"

He gave me a lopsided smile. "Only a little. But seriously, if the Wall is keeping the Talanagi, the most powerful creatures, from entering our territory of the Wilds, we should rip it down."

I nodded. "It will also make us more vulnerable to invasion through that area."

"We can handle that," he said confidently. "Especially with more soldiers bonded to Talanagi."

I really hoped this idea worked and didn't just send a bunch of Lottery winners out to die. They were all going to want to bond the best and most powerful, but not all would. It was a risk.

"Alright, head back to Sky Reach and rip down that wall. I'll oversee the early Lottery," I told him.

He saluted me, and I felt a genuineness from him that he wanted to follow my lead, and trusted me.

Before he left, I hooked him by the arm and pulled his ear close to me. "I killed Maxim's sister. She's on the other side of the park. Have two men bury her in an unmarked grave and expect retaliation."

He peered at me with surprise.

If Elaine were here, she would tell me to send her head back to Maxim with a threatening note, but I didn't want to stoke the fires anymore. Truth was, Maxim's unpredictability scared me. He said I would have three months, and he'd attacked in two. If I wanted to beat him, I'd have to be just as unpredictable. Once he heard I killed his sister, I had no doubt he would retaliate.

"Everyone, back to base! Leave is over," Commander Ledger barked. "Be on alert for a follow-up attack!"

People scattered then as the rain fell even harder around us. I peered up to see Colt on his griffin. The fire was nearly completely out.

Tetra rode Ariyel as she walked up beside me. "How can I help?" she asked.

I sighed, peering over at my bestie. "I'm calling an emergency Lottery. It's going to be chaos. People won't be fully ready. Help me manage it all, while still taking nights to go through my father's office?"

I hoped it wasn't too much to ask.

She nodded. "You got it."

I glanced down at her foot. "How is it?"

She sighed, and I saw the vulnerability in her gaze. "Days like today, I want to cut it off."

She'd said that before, but only once. A doctor she'd consulted with once had told her the painful flares would be gone with amputation, that a clean cut was better than what she was dealing with, but it would greatly impact her mobility. A wheelchair was an option. Or our scientists were just coming out with decent prosthetics. But there was no guarantee she would ever walk again.

I put a hand on her shoulder. "It's a bad day. It will pass."

She nodded, and the rain fell down her cheeks so hard I couldn't tell if she was crying or not.

'Kohen and Onyx are here,' Liana said, and the hairs on the back of my neck rose sharply.

'What? Where?' I spun in a circle, scanning the crowd.

'They are a ten-minute flight from here, in a small park. Do you want to see him?'

Tetra was looking at me like I'd grown two heads, probably because I'd just stopped talking and was now wide-eyed.

'Yes.' I wanted to cleave his head from his shoulders!

"I gotta go. Sleep at the house with the girls?" I asked her.

She nodded, frowning. "You okay?"

I looked over at the people still lingering, talking about entering the emergency Lottery, and nodded. "Tell you later."

When I walked over to Liana and slid my leg over her, she took to the skies.

'Your powers don't work on Kohen,' she reminded me.

He was impervious to fire and now could apparently block my thrall powers.

'Do you think he will try to hurt me?'

'No,' came her immediate answer.

'He killed me the last time I saw him,' I reminded her.

'I don't think he will ever do that again, and he only did it because he saw you surviving in a vision.'

I hated that she was on his side.

'I'm on your side, young one. But I can tell you, when I look at Kohen and you together and I see his energy... he loves you. Truly.'

That tore a hole right into my bandaged heart. *'He thinks he does. Killing my father isn't love.'*

Unless it *was* to save my life, but even then, it was messed up.

'He thinks he does,' she agreed.

'Do you forgive Onyx for what he did?' When I was attacked in the Wilds, Onyx attacked Liana and killed her.

'A mother always forgives her children, even if they are misguided and make mistakes.'

Well, Kohen wasn't my child, and there was no forgiveness in me for him yet. Not without proof of his outrageous claims.

'Why is he here? I told him not to come.'

'Onyx said he had a new vision.'

'I don't care,' I snapped at Liana, though I wasn't mad at her. *'I can't believe anything he says.'*

'Maybe just hear him out?' Liana offered.

'He can tell me through Onyx.'

'He is saying he wants to tell you in person.'

Of course he did. So he could manipulate me—and I was falling right into that trap, flying to see him with no backup. He could kill me again, and this time, maybe I wouldn't come back.

'Your power won't work on him, but I can still rip his throat out,' she assured me, causing me to smile.

We lowered ourselves into the thick vein of forest that ran along one of the more rural neighborhoods. I pulled my blade, feeling the anger I'd been carrying for Kohen rising in my chest.

As Liana broke through the trees and into the open meadow, I saw them. My heart stopped at the sight of Kohen peering up at me, Onyx off to the side.

I slipped off of Liana and jumped down, landing right behind Kohen. Lurching forward, I yanked him by the hair and pulled his back flush to my chest, holding my blade across his throat.

"Give me one reason," I growled, panting against his ear as adrenaline and rage coursed through me. But I knew it was a mistake to get this close to him the second I smelled him.

Ginger, cardamom... home.

"Maybe you should," he said, his voice filled with agony. "It would end my misery."

I rolled my eyes. "You don't get to wallow in any kind of pity, Kohen. You killed my father and me. You *disgust* me."

He nodded. "Not as much as I disgust myself."

I released my blade and shoved him away from me. He spun, letting me really see him for the first time. What I saw shocked me.

He'd lost a little weight, there were dark circles under his eyes like he hadn't slept, and his arms were all bandaged.

"What happened to your arms?" I asked.

He sighed. "Pulled a mother and child from a burning building two nights ago. Still healing."

I narrowed my eyes, trying to detect his lies.

"You're impervious to fire," I stated, calling his BS.

He looked at me blankly and then unwrapped one of his arms. I hissed when I saw four deep gashes. "But not to glass," he stated.

If he was insinuating that the mother and child had been in a fire that *we* started, well, I wasn't about to feel bad. That was war. He should have thought about that before he killed my father.

But I *did* feel bad. Deeply.

"Are the mother and child okay?" I asked.

He nodded.

I was falling for his crap again. He probably made that whole story up, even cut his own arms to get me to feel sorry for him.

"Why did you call me here?" I asked quickly, wanting to leave, wanting to look away from those deep blue eyes I had once lost myself in.

Kohen peered away from me like he couldn't meet my gaze, and my stomach sank.

"My gift has... matured. I see multiple timelines now. A dozen variations based on certain decision points. Not just the most likely one like I used to."

I snapped my fingers. I was not here to have a full-on conversation with him. "Okay, what was your vision? I have a country to run, and our ceasefire is ending soon."

He looked hurt at how cold I was being, but I didn't care.

"Don't freak out. We can still change it—"

"We!" I laughed. "Kohen, there will never be a *we* again."

He looked like I'd stabbed him in the chest. "Don't say that. Please."

"You're delusional if you think you can just kill my father, kill me, and I'd ever kiss you again—you are literally insane."

His bottom lip shook, and I honestly thought he was going to cry for a second until a mask of anger washed over him so hard and fast I wasn't prepared for it.

"Maybe I should have left him alive," Kohen said, stepping closer to me. "Maybe I should have let your father kill you. Then, at least you would have died loving me and knowing the truth."

"I hate you!" I screamed into his face as tears filled my eyes. "I hate that I can't trust anything you say."

"And I love you!" he yelled back. "I hate that you are so brainwashed you actually think my father was a bad man, and yours was good."

His words hurt, but at this point, I was numb inside.

"Just tell me what you saw so that I can go home, Kohen." I wanted to get the hell out of here. This hadn't gone as I'd planned. I was emotional and no longer had the upper hand.

He tried to step closer, and I stepped back. He nodded as if he should have expected that.

"In one vision, I saw Valor and her new bonded dead."

I gasped, bile rising in my throat. Of all the things I thought he would say, I never expected that.

"In another, I saw Victory taken hostage to Luska instead of Valor killed," he stated as if that would be a better option.

My heart rattled my ribcage like a drum. "Please tell me there was a third option," I whimpered.

His face went slack, and his eyes lost their brightness. "There is a scenario where I see all of your sisters living until they have gray hair and children of their own."

"Oh, thank the stars!" I breathed. "How do I get that version of events to come true?" I begged him.

There was agony written across his face then. "You marry Maxim Vlek." His voice was void of emotion.

His words were shocking, and I let them linger for a moment.

'There has to be another way. Ask him,' Liana growled into my mind. I knew how she felt about Maxim, that he was evil. In no way did I want to marry him, ever.

"Liana wants to know if there is any other way," I asked Kohen.

He looked up at me with a fire in his eyes. "I'll make a way."

I scoffed. That wasn't realistic.

I saw Kohen's gaze linger on the gold band on my finger. He swallowed hard.

"Did you read my letters?" he asked.

I shrugged. "Some of them."

Why was I still here? I should leave. He'd told me what I needed to know. I should fly home and lock all three of my sisters in the underground base at Sky Reach.

"Are you at least looking for the truth about your father?" Kohen asked, "Or have you just given up on me, on us?"

I didn't know why that question affected me so deeply. A sob formed in my throat, and I had to choke it down.

"Kohen," I said through my emotion, "I gave up on us the night I found out that you killed my father in cold blood and then held me while I cried about it. If you love someone, you don't cause them that kind of pain. It's selfish."

Kohen closed his eyes, dropping to his knees and hanging his head as if deep in prayer, as if the weight of my words had just physically struck him.

'I want to go now,' I told Liana. She moved behind me, where she'd been talking to Onyx. I slid my leg over her, and Kohen glanced up at me. What I saw in his eyes scared me. He looked dead inside.

"I hope you find out the truth about your father. A truth even I can't tell you, or you would never believe me. A truth so dark it would make you want to have killed him yourself."

I rolled my eyes, and Liana kicked off the ground, heading for my sister's house. He was such a good liar, so good with the dramatics.

'What truth is he talking about?' I asked Liana.

'I don't know, but his energy looks like he's on death's door,' she admitted.

I shouldn't feel bad for him, but I did.

I had too many things to worry about right now, and Kohen Badshah was the least of them.

CHAPTER TWELVE

Aisling

THE SECOND I got back to my house, Elaine was waiting in the living room.

"Another attack in Riverine!" she said right when I walked in.

I nodded. "Get ready to take notes. We have a lot of work to do."

She perked up at that, taking out a notepad and pen as I walked her over to our dining table. She sat down, but I paced.

"First, send all three of my sisters to Sky Reach to live

twenty-four-seven in the underground bunker with round-the-clock guards."

Elaine raised an eyebrow at that.

"I'll tell you later," I said. There was too much on my mind, too many boxes to check off.

"Then send out a mass invitation to all households with citizens aged eighteen to twenty-five. We are inviting them to join an emergency Lottery which will be held in two days' time. They need to have a three-day pack and be ready to serve their country."

If possible, Elaine's eyebrows grew higher.

"Make sure that includes people from past Lotteries who didn't get in, like Charlene," I added.

Elaine peered up at me. "Do you want me to make sure Charlene's name is called?"

My father had done it with Kohen and Jace and who knows how many people. But I wanted to do things by the rules.

"No, but let's pick three times as many names as we normally would."

"I have to counsel you against that. We don't want to thin the creature population faster than they can reproduce."

She hadn't heard.

"Commander Ledger is ripping down the wall in the Wilds as we speak to allow the Talanagi into our side. There will be plenty of creatures."

Her mouth popped open, and she grinned. "Okay, Empress. What else?" She was feverishly taking notes.

I told her we needed to get the training center up and

running, and to have Sergeant Ashendell be in charge of all trainees' boot camp. I was sticking with people I trusted here.

"Post Tetra at the training center while the kids go through boot. If there is an attack, I need her to shield it."

There were notes upon notes as we stayed up into the early hours of the morning, planning things for my country to try to keep it above water.

"And the one-week truce with Imbria?" Elaine said. "After one week, are we... resuming?" she asked.

"I don't know. Ask me when a week has passed." I hated that I hadn't just killed Kohen where he stood a few hours ago.

"And are we retaliating on Luska for the attack?" she asked.

"I did. I killed Maxim's sister, and we are cutting down the wall and luring the Talanagi to our side to bond with our fleet. I think that's enough for now, but we need to be ready for bombs to rain. Activate all reserve Fleet personnel back to their bases."

Elaine wrote that down. "How are we luring the Talanagi to our side?" she asked.

I sighed, rubbing my temples. "I don't know, but you and I have forty-eight hours to figure that out before the Lottery."

Elaine stood. "I'll put on a pot of coffee."

I reached out and grasped her hand, and she froze, looking over at me.

I gave her a soft smile. "There is no one I would rather have by my side as I run the country in a crisis than you."

She pointed a finger at me. "Don't get all mushy. I raised a warrior," she joked with a wink.

I saluted her in mock fashion, and she squeezed my hand. "I thank the stars your father hired me all those years ago. This was as close as I would ever get to being a mother." There was a bit of sadness in her voice, like maybe she wanted kids, but it had never happened for whatever reason.

"Well, good, because we thank the stars for you, too, and we think of you as a mother. You know that, right?"

Her eyes filled with tears, and she smacked my hand. "Don't make me cry, Aisling Everhart."

I grinned, and she went to make the coffee, wiping her eyes.

I sat down, letting a bit of gratitude wash over me. The days to come were going to be filled with stress and anxiety, but for this one moment, I was choosing to be thankful for all I had. My three sisters were safely asleep in this house. So was my best friend. And Elaine was by my side through it all.

I had to believe that I could turn things around.

My country was depending on me.

In the end, it was Liana who helped us find a way to lure the Talanagi to our side. With food. She said a favorite of the flying creatures was a certain kind of rabbit that we had plentifully growing in the hillsides of Riverine. We captured as many as we could and released them in the northern end of our Wilds and then watched at night as the creatures, both Talanagi and regular ones, came over the border to our side.

The war had resumed with Luska, mostly just on the Wall. They were pissed we'd torn part of it down and were shooting Sky Reach with projectile weapons every chance they got. My sisters were safe underground there, with strict instructions not to leave, and I was in Riverine about to preside over my first Lottery.

It wasn't supposed to happen like this. It was supposed to be only at age nineteen and only once in your life. But we needed soldiers, and there weren't enough nineteen-year-olds ready. Plus, I never thought it was fair you couldn't enter a second time if you weren't picked. All in all, we had ten thousand enter the Lottery. We were packed to the gills inside, with the doors open and speakers that would blast the names called outside.

After the Fleet anthem played, Elaine peered over at me, and I nodded, walking over to the podium. I peered out at the amassed crowd of young people all around my age and stood tall. "Unprecedented times call for unprecedented measures," I called out. "I want to thank each and every one of you who volunteered today to have a chance to go into the Wilds and bond a creature. For your families and for our nation."

The crowd clapped cheerfully, and I waited until they quieted to keep going. "If we truly want a chance against Luksa, we need more Fleet soldiers to bond Talanagi!"

A hush fell over the crowd.

"The rumors you have probably heard are true. I bonded Liana in the Luskin Wilds!"

The crowd roared with chatter and talking, but I yelled over them. "Two nights ago, we broke down the wall to lure the Talanagi to our side. So, I am here to plead with you. If you think you have the strength within you to bond and survive a Talanagi, then please head north and do so. If you do not, then that's okay. We still need you, and there are plenty of powerful creatures waiting to bond."

The crowd erupted into applause and shouts of excitement, and I grinned.

"Good luck. I'll be rooting for you. Our entire country will."

The roar was deafening. Elaine had to yell two times to quiet everyone down. When she finally did, the names began to be called. I sat there for hours as each and every name was called. Whoops and cheers rang throughout the stadium, and people ran in from outside to claim their place on the stage. We filled the stage four times before we finally called an end to the event. About sixteen hundred new soldiers in all would fight for their lives tonight. I was praying at least a hundred made it out alive, and ten of them were riding Talanagi. The odds were brutal, and the deaths would be high, but now more than ever, we needed to fight, or I feared there would be no Amersea this time next year.

I walked among the chosen, whispering words of advice. *Stay awake. Drink caffeine. Form strong alliances. Don't give up*. By the time I reached the buses, everyone was loading up, and I was reminded of when I met Kohen. The way he'd told me he'd take care of Jace for me. The way he'd bowed out of the alliance just so I would join it and look after his friends.

"You did great." Alek's deep voice called beside me, and I jumped a little, pulled from my thoughts.

He smiled. "Sorry."

I waved him off. "I was reminiscing from our time in there." I watched more and more soldiers load up on the buses.

"We were lucky to have each other," he stated.

Charlene walked past me, grinning with her three-day backpack on, and I stepped out and stopped her.

"Empress." She saluted me. I was glad her name was called.

I leaned into her ear. "Don't underestimate yourself in there. You should get a group of the strongest and go for the Talanagi."

When I pulled back, her grin grew wider. "I plan on it, Empress. I'll fly out, or they'll bring me out in a body bag."

She deserved this. She should have been chosen before.

"I'm happy for you," I told her.

"Thanks," she said and then got on the bus.

When I slipped back to stand next to Alek, I felt his gaze on me and turned to face him. What I saw made me a little uncomfortable. He was peering at me with adoration, a deep longing in his gaze.

"You did amazing in there," he told me. "Do you want to have dinner together?"

"I can't," I said too quickly, trying to ignore the hurt that crossed his face. I wasn't ready for what he wanted from me. I wasn't sure I would ever be.

"I have a date with Tetra," I added, and he nodded.

Trying to rifle through my father's old files and find out if he tried to murder me, I wanted to say.

"Alright, well... I'll see you soon." He shuffled awkwardly and then leaned forward to kiss my cheek. I flinched a little, hating that I was in this fake arrangement with him, but he had real feelings, and I could, too. If Jace hadn't ripped my heart out, and Kohen hadn't ran it over with a train. I was too broken inside for anything real with him, and I felt like I might have led him on the other night. But before I could say anything about it, he was gone.

I sighed.

Elaine joined me, and we both waited until the last bus left before Verik drove around with the car.

Elaine turned to face me, squeezing both of my shoulders. "I'll have Verik take me to Sky Reach and keep an eye on the girls. You do what you need to do with Tetra. I'll get you survival numbers as cadets start exiting the Wilds."

Survival numbers—because I'd just sent a bunch of young kids to their deaths. Liana descended from the sky, where she had been waiting, and I nodded to Elaine. "Keep me informed." I'd had a house phone installed so she could call me there. We couldn't speak about anything classified, as an operator could always be listening.

With that, I headed to my house to continue the dreaded investigation of my own father.

CHAPTER
THIRTEEN

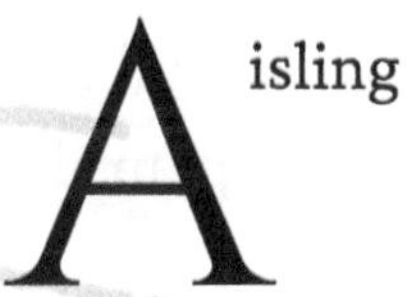isling

THE FIRST NIGHT of the Lottery candidates being in the Wilds, Tetra and I found nothing incriminating on my father. Into night two with no promising evidence, my anger for Kohen was brewing hotter and hotter with each passing minute.

He lied. I knew he lied.

I tore open the lid of a box of old notes and telephone messages and started to angrily rifle through them. But when I saw his handwriting on one note, I stilled. It was a copy of a message that he left with the operator to give to someone at the training center. There were coffee stains on it, but it clearly read.

Just get the job done.

My heart picked up speed in my chest.

"This could mean anything," I said out loud.

Tetra hobbled over to where I was and picked up the note in my hand, her eyebrows rising as she read.

"What do you think?" I asked.

She shrugged. "It could mean, 'get the job of killing my daughter done'. It could also mean, 'get the job of training those new recruits done'."

I sighed in relief, actually laughing that I'd been paranoid for a minute.

"Totally. That's what I thought."

Tetra frowned at me. "Do you really think your dad will have evidence lying around his office that he tried to kill his own daughter? Isn't that something he would plan in person?"

She was right. We had an operator phone system, and every phone call was monitored. I flashed to the day he drove me to boot camp. I'd been so proud he wanted to see me off, but then he'd almost left without saying goodbye. He was talking to some of the drill instructors.

"Kohen probably knows that. That's why he sent me on this wild goose chase when I should be at the training center or the Wilds ready to welcome our new recruits."

A few had already come out bonded—none to a Talanagi yet, but it was night two. This was when things really started happening in the Wilds.

Tetra grasped my hands. "Let's take a break. We can keep

going tomorrow after we hopefully have good news of how many cadets made it out."

I nodded, setting the note on my desk.

A single note after multiple nights of searching over a dozen boxes.

Kohen lied. The bastard lied!

As I was leaving the office, the phone rang.

I picked it up.

"Hello, this is Empress Aisling."

"Empress, I have Admiral Steele on the line for you."

Elaine? My heart sped up. Was everything with my sisters okay?

"Put her through," I told her.

There was a click, and then Elaine was on the line.

"Everything is fine," she started, and I relaxed.

"Except for the fact that we are dying of boredom!" Victory shrieked in the background, and I grinned.

"And I haven't even learned to properly fly on Zara because we are separated! It's torture!" Valor growled.

"I left my purple nail polish at home!" Virtue whined.

"They want to come home just for a night," Elaine told me, and I could tell by the fatigue in her voice that she was tired of their complaining.

"No letter from Maxim? No retaliation?" I asked.

"Nothing."

I killed his sister. It was eerie he wasn't responding.

"Have Verik drive them in a caravan of four cars. You and Vespa stay with them the entire time. They can come in the morning and stay one night. Then we all go back to Sky

Reach and move in together. I'll be done wrapping up the Lottery here by then."

Three excited teenager shrieks filled the line, and I smiled.

"We will see you tomorrow. I'll have Gwen hang back here. She's having fun with her old boot buddies," Elaine told me, and we both hung up.

I opened my mouth to tell Tetra, and she waved me off. "I heard everything. They are so loud. Remind me to only have quiet children."

I barked out in laughter at that. "Oh, T, I don't think it works that way."

We got washed up for bed and went to our respective rooms. I was exhausted, but my mind was chewing on that note.

Just get the job done.

Just get the job done.

Just get the job done.

That night, I dreamed of Kohen, of swollen kisses and whispered promises. It all felt so real that when I woke up, I was breathless and feeling empty inside.

If loving Kohen didn't kill me, his lies would.

TETRA AND I WOKE UP, made some breakfast, and looked through some boxes in the office for a couple of hours by the time the girls arrived. We only had three boxes left, and I was really starting to fear the end of this journey with no solid evidence.

"My purple nail polish! Bless the stars!" Virtue came out of her room clutching the tiny bottle like it was ember.

I snort-laughed. My gaze swept the room and landed on Valor, who was staring at Tetra's foot with a horror-stricken look on her face.

What the...?

Movement at the back door caused my gaze to peer out the back window to see Zara staring intently in the window at us.

"What's going on, Valor?" I asked my sister. She didn't look okay, and her creature normally stayed deeper in the yard with Liana.

Valor shook her head. "Nothing." She tore her gaze away from Tetra's foot and chewed on her lip.

Now even Tetra had seemed to notice. "Does my mangled foot bother you now, Val? I can put a sock over the ugly thing," she joked.

Valor looked pained. "No. It isn't that."

'Zara says Valor's gift is emerging, and she's fighting it,' Liana told me.

Oh, that made more sense.

"Val, can I speak to you in your room for a moment?" I asked.

She nodded, looking on the verge of tears, which was very off-brand for my stoic sister. She was the one made of steel, the one most like me.

Tetra caught my gaze as I passed, and I gave her a small smile.

'Did she say what the power might be?' I asked as we walked to Valor's room.

'No,' Liana said.

If Valor was about to display some firepower, I would want her outside.

The second we got into Valor's room, I shut the door, and she spun to face me. "It hurts," she whimpered, tears streaming down her face.

I gasped at the sudden change in her. "What hurts? Where?" I peered over her body, looking for injuries.

She lifted her right socked foot and began to massage it.

I frowned. "Did you get injured?"

Valor's chest heaved up and down as she fought to keep control of her emotions. She shook her head.

"Then how does it—?" My eyes widened.

That was the same foot as Tetra's.

"Valor, do you think you can pick up on people's pain? Take it away?" Those healers were extremely rare, but completely removing pain was such a valuable asset to the Fleet.

"I think I can do more than that." Her voice cracked. "I think I can heal it."

Oh.

I reached out and grasped her shoulders. "That's so very sweet, Val, but Tetra has seen a healer. They said she was born with it, and it couldn't be healed. It's a birth deformity, not an injury."

Valor's lip quivered. "But I think I can heal it," she said again.

'Something is happening out here,' Liana said, and my eyes widened.

I tore open the door and ran back out to the living room. Everyone stood in awe as they stared at the back glass patio door. Zara was standing there, but there were arcs of gold light splashing off of her. Ariyel was outside with Liana, watching from a ways off.

I spun, peering at Tetra.

Elaine was very quiet, Victory and Virtue speechless beside her.

"Valor thinks she can heal your foot," I blurted out to my bestie.

Tetra's mouth popped open. "It's not possible. I was told that as a child."

Valor stepped into the room, staring at her hands. There were the same golden arcs of light coming off of her palms.

I gasped.

"Let Zara inside now!" Valor snapped at me.

Something was happening. And even though I was empress, and she was my little sister, I did as she commanded. Because if there was even a small chance that my best friend could be freed of years of crippling pain, I was taking it.

I yanked the back door open and started shoving chairs out of the way to make room for the small dragon to come inside.

Tetra swallowed hard, staring at Valor in shock.

"It might do nothing. It might just take your pain away.

Or she might be misreading the power," I told Tetra as both Zara and Valor approached her.

Valor shook her head as if to argue with me. "No," was all she said.

No. Just that.

"But—"

"Shhh," Elaine scolded me, and I fell silent.

Stars, let Valor be right. Let Tetra be healed.

CHAPTER FOURTEEN

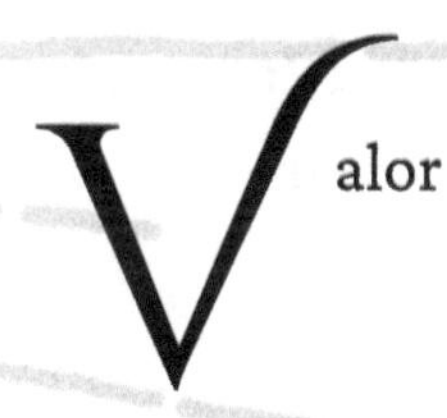

Valor

For days, I'd been feeling foot pain around Tetra. It took me a while to put two and two together, and now I knew. Her pain was calling to me. I'd been around a couple of other injured people at Sky Reach. Just passing by them in the hall, their pain called to me, too, so I ran quickly to get away. But Tetra... I couldn't ignore the pleas of her body any longer. The muscles, tendons, nerves, and bones were all crying out to be healed. That was the other creepy thing. I knew what tendons felt like, what they looked like without skin. All in my head. I could see it. I'd been seeing Tetra's twisted foot in my mind's eye for days, begging me to resculpt it like an artist with clay. It terrified me, so I'd ignored it. I ignored Zara's inquiries about it, too. But I couldn't ignore them any longer. Now, I was one hundred percent certain I could heal her foot. I just didn't know the cost. Would it take from me? The energy had to come from somewhere. I knew that, too, instinctively.

Aisling didn't believe it. She was watching Zara and me skeptically as we approached Tetra. Golden arcs of color lit up the living room walls as I walked toward her.

'Is this healing magic?' I asked Zara about the gold.

'I suspect so. It is not a magic I had before bonding you,' she told me.

It seemed whatever I was about to do, I needed Zara with me, because she had more of the golden stuff coming off of her than I did.

"Lie down," I told Tetra, moving the tendons and bones in my mind's eye from her mangled foot. It was as if someone had taken an x-ray of her deformity and then placed it into my head. But instead of a black-and-white x-ray, this had blood vessels and tendons, each one moving out of the way, twisting and turning into the right order as I worked through it like a math problem.

Tetra plopped onto the ground, wincing as she pulled her slightly swollen, red foot out before me. A sharp pang of pain hit my right foot, and I grimaced at the same time Tetra did.

"Don't try this if it will hurt you," Tetra told me as the pain in my right foot got worse, throbbing like a heartbeat, each time with more agony.

"It already hurts," I told her. "How have you lived like this for so long?" I asked, and tears filled her eyes.

The picture of her foot in my mind's eye finally reached perfection, and I sighed in relief as if I'd just worked out the worst mathematical problem Elaine had ever given me.

"What do you mean?" Tetra peered at the way I kept off of my right foot, holding it up slightly to dull the aching.

Crouching down beside her, I could hear the room holding their collective breath. Zara stepped closer, too. The bands of golden light glowing on Tetra's face now.

"T, if this hurts me, it's worth it," I told her. Then I placed my golden-glowing hands on her hot right foot—the image in my mind snapped as an earth-shattering pain splintered in my foot, breaking it into a thousand pieces.

Golden light exploded off of Zara, too, blinding the entire room momentarily. Then Tetra and I both screamed as the pain became too much, and blackness took me.

CHAPTER
FIFTEEN

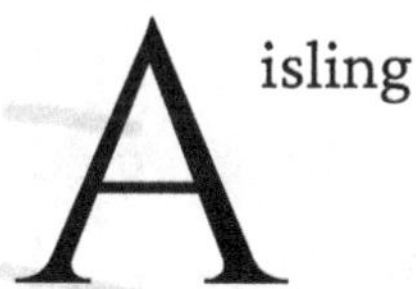

isling

“Val!” I shook my little sister as panic washed over me. “Tetra!” I reached over and shook her, too.

“They’re dead!” Victory sobbed.

I peered at the rise and fall of their chests. At Zara, who was still alive beside me.

“No one is dead,” I snapped.

That’s when my gaze fell to Tetra’s foot.

“Stars!” I skittered backwards.

In all the years I’d known Tetra, her right foot looked like it had been twisted up in a blender.

But now… it was… like mine.

Valor's eyes snapped open, and then so did Tetra's.

I reached down and yanked the sock off of Valor's right foot, fully afraid that she had somehow magically taken the injury on herself, but when I saw her regular-looking foot with purple, chipped toenail paint, I laughed.

Pure joy ripped through me. Even Elaine was smiling.

"It can't be," Elaine said.

Tetra looked over at me, confused, as if coming out of a dream. I peered at Valor, who was staring at Tetra's foot and then at Zara. She grinned.

"Are you okay? How are you feeling?" I asked Valor.

"I'm totally fine," she said.

"You passed out, you're not fine!" I told her.

An ear-splitting sob ripped from Tetra's throat, and I turned to see her staring at her foot in shock. She wiggled her ankle, then her toes. It was crazy, after so many years of seeing her foot twisted and red, to find the appendage perfect and without flaw.

"Valor..." Tetra managed between sobs and then pulled my sister in for a hug.

I stood back. Then we all watched as Valor slowly helped Tetra stand. It was the moment of truth. Could she walk? Run? Would it hurt? Would she still limp? A thousand thoughts went through my head.

Tetra bent down to Zara and held the creature's gaze.

"Thank you," she said. Then Tetra smiled, and I knew Zara must have responded.

Tetra was standing on one foot, waiting to try her "new foot" out, and I braced myself for how heartbreaking it would be if it wasn't a full healing. Virtue snuggled into Elaine's side as Tetra put a small amount of weight on the foot. Her eyes flew wide. Then, she took two steps without a limp or a drag.

Again, she wept, breaking down, and I couldn't bear it anymore. I pulled her into my arms as she cried like a baby.

"Is it healed? Fully?" I asked.

She could only nod.

I pulled away from her, smiling, and then Victory dashed behind Tetra, smacking her back. "Tag, you're it!" She raced past Valor's creature and out the open back door.

Tetra looked frozen for a second, then a wild grin took over her face. She bolted after Victory, clumsily at first, like she'd never run before in her life.

Because she hadn't. Not really. Not without a cane and a dragging limb behind her.

I peered at Valor, my throat clenching with emotion.

"Do you have any idea how special you are?" I asked as I approached her.

She shrugged. "I'm not a warrior. I'll probably never be empress now. A healer is just... boring."

"That's not true," Elaine scolded Valor as Virtue dashed out of the house to chase Tetra as well. It appeared that my bestie was very slow and not well-versed in tag. Even Ariyel had joined in on the fun, running around with Vespa as well.

Victory was winning, but Tetra was laughing in joy and running around the yard like a child. It brought tears to my eyes, and I turned back to face my sister.

"Of course, it's not true! You'll be the greatest empress

this country has ever seen," I told her. "Do you have any idea what kind of peace and joy you could bring to this nation if you could take away all disease and deformity and illness? The little babies born with bent limbs, tucked-in lips, the people suffering from incurable diseases. Valor, your power is incredible." I had to clear my throat to keep from getting emotional.

Zara nuzzled Valor's leg as if in agreement with me.

Valor looked a little more excited now that I'd said that, but then her face fell.

"What is it?" Elaine asked her, walking closer to be near her.

"In what world can I ever bring peace and healing and joy to our nation when we are constantly at war?"

It was like a knife to my chest. Because she was right. Amersea's entire existence was fueled by war. Right now, I had over a thousand young Amerseans fighting for their lives just for the chance to bond a creature and fight in the Fleet. To die for the Fleet. It's how it had always been.

I peered out at Tetra, awkwardly running as Victory and Virtue chased her laughing, and I wondered if there was any possibility I could give my people a future without war. If there were some way to bring peace to our nation.

CHAPTER
SIXTEEN

Aisling

THE GIRLS and Elaine were asleep, and Tetra and I were in the office going through papers. With only one box left, it was starting to feel really dismal. We both stared at it. The office looked like a tornado had ripped through it, papers and yellow file folders everywhere. Maps of Luksa and Imbria and different war strategies for hypothetical situations that had never happened were strewn all over the place. But nothing that proved my father paid anyone to try to kill me.

"I'm going in. This is it. Then we eat dessert and sleep," Tetra announced, walking over to the box on her newly healed foot. I stopped her, forcing her to face me.

"How are you dealing with all that?" I pointed to her foot. She'd been acting so casually, almost like nothing happened.

She grinned. "How am I dealing with a lifelong, painful disability suddenly being gone? I'm doing amazing."

I laughed at that. I didn't know what I expected. More tears? Therapy?

Her face did betray some deeper emotion then. "I'll never be able to fully thank Valor for what she did."

I nodded. "I don't think she quite understands how special she is." She was too young to grasp something of this magnitude—only angry she wasn't a warrior.

"I can't believe that little booger who used to draw on our faces when we were asleep was the one to change my life so drastically." She wiggled her foot again as if making sure the healing was real.

I smiled and found myself wondering if any of the cadets who came out of the Wilds would have a similar gift. What a world we could live in if we had a hundred more like my sister.

Tetra called me out for my procrastination: "You're delaying opening the final box."

I chuckled dryly. "On one hand, whatever is in that box means my own father tried to kill me. On the other, it means a man I loved so deeply lied to me from the very first kiss."

Tetra nodded. "Let's find out which it is. Together."

Taking a steadying breath, I nodded, and we lifted the lid.

Right from the beginning, I knew this box was different.

Inside was a metal box the same size as the cardboard, only slightly smaller to fit inside.

"Interesting. It's a safe or something." Tetra reached in and heaved it out, grunting as I pulled away the outer shell.

When it was on the floor, I noticed the front had a key lock.

"Dang, no key," I growled.

Tetra rolled her eyes. "We are *not* letting that stop us. I'll be right back."

When she came back, she was holding a crowbar from the storage shed. I gave her an impressed look as she wedged it between the lock and the box.

"Don't wake the girls. That's the last thing I need right now."

She grunted, moving left and right, until finally, with a crack that caused both of us to freeze, the lock busted open.

My pulse raced as Tetra removed the twisted lock and opened the metal lid. Safes were for keeping secrets. What secrets did my father want to hide in here? I wondered.

Tetra began to pull out files and maps and papers and we sat down, both a little more serious than before.

I peered at one map, confused by what I was seeing, until I realized it was a map of the old train station that ran under Emberlane Park. With it was a table of times. Circled were the busiest times when thousands would be on board coming from work in the city and going home out into the suburbs. The next was a paper showing the transformers that ran our city's lighting system and the giant ember that fueled it.

"Aisling..." Tetra's voice broke, and I peered up to see horror written on her expression. She handed me a stack of papers with a shaky fist, and I pulled them from her.

What in the world?

It was directions on how to make a homemade bomb.

Why would my dad have maps of the subway? And the lighting system, and how to make a bomb? My heart beat so wildly that dizziness washed over me. Then I found a piece of paper in my father's handwriting.

We can call it the Great Blackout. Blame Imbria. Kill Badshah. Take over. Double our land.

I screamed, throwing the paper as I fell backward.

"What?" Tetra leaned forward, picking up the paper and reading it. As she did, I watched a mask of anger slide over her face.

"Aisling, if your dad killed thousands of his own people... that's unforgivable."

"I know." I barely recognized my own voice. Kohen was right—he'd been right all along.

Her mask of anger softened. "I'm sorry." She reached for me, but I pulled back. I felt dirty. I was a byproduct of him. His spawn. What if I turned evil, too? Maybe I already was. I'd killed the red rider in a sick way that I still couldn't wipe from my mind.

Tetra grabbed the sides of my face and forced me to look at her. "I know what you're thinking. You're nothing like him."

My bottom lip shook. "What if I am?" I asked.

Tetra shook her head. "You're not. You and your sisters are not."

There was a finality in her tone. She had spoken, and that was that.

She released me. "Ash, you know what this means, right?"

My hands shook. I was still processing everything.

"Kohen was right." My voice felt foreign to my own ears. "I called his father a terrorist." Tears leaked from my eyes. I couldn't believe how much I'd cried the past few months. More than in my whole life.

I felt like I was unraveling.

"We all did," Tetra said. "Because of this. Propaganda. We believed the papers, the investigation, our emperor."

I swallowed hard. "How do I fix this? If I show people this to clear Kohen's father's name, they'll think my family name is tainted. They'll hang me."

Tetra nodded. "I think you need to let the past be the past for now. But there is something you can fix, someone I think you owe an apology to. I think Kohen saved your life, Aisling. As painful as it was, in the way he did it..."

I nodded. The tears hadn't stopped. I was questioning how anyone could have this much water in their body.

"I've said too many awful things to him. I've bombed half his country and burned most of it, too." I shook my head. "He won't forgive me."

"Why don't you let him say that or not?"

"I can't face him. I'm ashamed of what my father did." I hugged my arms. "I'm ashamed of how I acted."

"You didn't know. He should have found a way to prove this to you without killing your father."

I shook my head. "I wouldn't have listened. My father was my idol. I'm just now realizing that."

"Go to Kohen. Tell him what you know and take it from there," she said.

We stood, and I pulled her in for a hug and wiped at my cheeks, finally feeling the tears subside.

"I love you," I told her.

"I love you, too." I could hear the smile in her voice.

When I pulled back, she was beaming.

"What?" I asked.

She shrugged. "I like who you've become without your father. You're a strong, self-assured woman."

"Aww," I joked and pinched her cheeks like a grandmother would. She rolled her eyes.

"I'll wake you the second I get home," I told her.

"You better!" she called out as I ran to the back door to see if Liana was still in the backyard.

'Liana, I need you to contact Kohen.'

'I already have. I told him you want to meet. He said to come to him. I know where they are. Some village in Imbria.'

Imbria? That was dangerous for me. His people would likely kill me if they saw me.

'He said he's alone but for one other. You will be safe. He promised.'

Was he expecting me? Did he know I was coming to apologize?

Nerves ate at my stomach as I walked outside, my mind

still spinning with the fact that my father was responsible for the murder of thousands of Amerseans. And worse, he'd pinned it on someone else in order to take over their country.

Kohen's dad was killed because of a lie. Kohen lost his right to the crown and the nice life he and his brothers should have had because of my father.

Lies. Lies. Lies. That's all I'd been sold my entire life.

'You're smoking,' Liana said.

I looked down at the skin of my arms, and sure enough, she was right. I felt like I would explode with rage. Had my father been alive right now, I would have killed him myself.

All those families. Remembrance Day. The war on Imbria. The lengths to which my father went to, for what? Double the ember and some extra land. It wasn't worth the cost of even one life.

I was flitting in and out from rage to sorrow. When I reached Liana, she nuzzled me, and I stroked her neck.

'I can't believe it. I'm in shock,' was all I said as I hopped up onto her back and settled into the saddle.

'I can,' she stated brutally and kicked off the ground.

That hurt. The fact that she knew my father was capable of something like this and I was too brainwashed to have even considered it made me feel raw.

'I'm sorry,' she amended. *'If you could see energy like I do, you would understand.'*

'And Kohen's energy is good?'

'Yes,' she stated simply.

'And my father's was bad?'

'Yes. But nothing near as evil as Maxim's.'

That sent a chill up my spine. I felt like my entire life that I'd lived with a monster, and everyone saw it but me.

We flew in silence for a long time; me, stuck in my thoughts. I replayed every time my father gave a speech on Remembrance Day to the victims' families. How he used the attack that he created to control our people and take more land that wasn't his. I cried. I nearly threw up. I screamed. All the while, Liana just flew in quiet companionship.

I thought of all the times Kohen tried to convince me of the truth, from day one in the Wilds when I'd said those awful things about his father. Even Anika knew. All the times Kohen had said he would protect me no matter what. That he would even lie to protect me.

He'd done exactly that. Deep shame washed over me as we flew over Imbria. The fires had mostly been put out since we had called a temporary peace, but the damage was done. Trees and villages burned. For what?

A lie.

A lie that burned its way through an entire country.

I could never fix this. *This* was unforgivable.

'We're close,' Liana told me.

'I don't know if I can face him,' I told her, wondering if we should turn back. This was too big a thing to apologize for. Kohen and I felt like we were on opposite sides of a deep cavern. What would I even say to him?

I'm sorry my dad pinned the murder of thousands of people on your father and killed him and then took over your country and enslaved your brothers into poverty. Meanwhile, I defended him the entire time, and then he tried to kill me, and you took care of the problem, and I burned your country for it.

No. No. I couldn't.

'Liana, turn back.' Tears fell down my cheeks as the wind whipped past and carried them away.

'We're here, little one. I think this will help you heal. To see him.'

No, this would gut me. But maybe I needed that. Maybe I should let Kohen ream me out for everything and get it off his chest. It would make him feel better. That, I could give him. That was the only thing I could give him. A humble apology. A, *'you were right'*.

Liana landed over a small half-burned village, still smoking from the recently-put-out fires.

Kohen was there, leaning up against a brick wall, speaking to an older man in a ceremonial dress. A priest? Probably there to bury the dead that I burned.

When Liana landed, the priest nodded to Kohen and then left down a dark alley.

I swallowed hard, no longer caring if this was a trap. If Kohen had lured me here to ambush me and kill me.

I felt like I could barely breathe under the shame of this guilt I carried. Without meeting his gaze, I slipped off Liana, head down as I wiped my cheeks and walked over to him. When his shoes came into view, I dropped to my knees before him, head bowed, tears falling from my cheeks onto his dusty black boots.

"You were right," I managed to croak out. "Your father didn't cause the Great Blackout. Mine did. I know what I've done is unforgivable, but I want you to know I will live with the mistake of giving my father blind loyalty for the rest of my life. I'm sorry."

Silence. He said nothing.

He could take my head right now, and I would deserve it. He could knee me in the face and walk away and bomb our country for ten nights straight, and I would do nothing.

But he didn't.

He crouched down, grasping my face with the sides of his hands, and forced me to look up at him.

Why the hell was he smiling?

He registered the alarm on my face and laughed.

"You're laughing?" Had he gone insane? Had I driven him to insanity?

He glanced at my lips and back into my eyes.

"I had two visions this morning of this moment. In one, you kneel before me pretending to apologize, and then slit my throat, saying you found no evidence of wrongdoing on your father."

I gasped.

"In the other, you kneel and actually apologize. I wasn't sure which I was going to get. I love you, Aisling, but you never would have believed me, or Anika, or anyone, if we told you that your father planted the terrorist attack on my father to gain ember and land. You had to find out yourself."

He stood, pulling me up with him, and I was so shocked at how normal he was being that I couldn't speak.

"I love you," he said again, running his finger over my lips. "I forgive you."

Tears spilled out from my eyes, running down my face. Who had I become to cry this much? What was wrong with me?

I shook my head. "I don't deserve it."

"Yes, you do," he whispered against my mouth, leaning forward to crush my lips in a passionate kiss. I whimpered as the familiar taste of Kohen splashed across my tongue. Walking forward until his back hit the wall, I boxed him in, pressing my entire body against his. Our tongues stroked each other as I ate up the affection I'd felt starved for these last few months without him. I breathed him in, moaning against his mouth as heat built in my core.

All I could feel right now was pure gratitude that he accepted my apology.

When we both pulled away, we were breathless, grinning. Somehow, the war, the lies, the betrayal, it had faded away, and I was just in a love bubble with Kohen—the only thing that seemed real.

"Marry me," he said suddenly, and it felt like the rug was pulled out from under me.

I laughed softly. "Kohen... I'm engaged to Alek." I held up my left hand to show the ring.

Reaching out, he pulled the ring off my finger and tucked it into my pocket. Then he pulled something shiny from his and dropped to his knee.

I gasped.

Taking my hand, he held a gorgeous ring before me. It was a pink sapphire surrounded by small green emeralds in a yellow-gold band.

"This was my mother's. I've dreamed of giving it to you since you first kissed me at graduation. I've seen us married, Aisling. Our love saves Amersea and Imbria from total annihilation at Luska's hands."

I shook my head, tears building back in my eyes. "My people would never allow it, Kohen. They will disown me, my sisters. They aren't ready for this."

"Are you?" he asked.

My heart ached at the question.

"If your people were not in the equation. Would you? Tonight? Marry me?"

Tonight? My mouth popped open. "The priest?" I asked, indicating the man he'd been speaking to earlier.

Kohen grinned. "He's waiting to wed us, if you say yes. So I will ask you one more time. Aisling Everhart, will you be my wife?"

I did something selfish then, without consulting my advisors and without thinking of my sisters or my country. I did something for myself.

"Yes," I breathed.

His grin grew wider as he slipped the ring onto my finger. Then he stood, placing another kiss on my lips. I'd never felt so complete as when Kohen's lips were on mine. "Stars, I missed you, Aisling," he breathed against my mouth, and I whimpered.

I'd missed him too—I'd missed *us*. I'd prayed that our love wasn't fake. Something in my heart healed at that moment. Sometimes, our parents disappointed us. My mother died, not her fault, but it had left me looking for attention and approval from the only remaining parent I had left. Which meant I'd glanced past all of my father's faults until, in the end, he let me down, too. Now Kohen filled those gaps. Healed the wounds that an absent narcissist had inflicted. I didn't know if I could ever truly show him how much that meant to me, but if binding myself to him in marriage now meant that I could spend the rest of my life feeling this way, feeling healed and loved and good enough, then I was saying yes and never looking back.

Kohen pulled my hand, guiding me down the small dark alley the priest had disappeared into, and when we came out the other side, I grinned.

The small outdoor patio was still standing, beauty among the ashes of a fallen place. An arch trellis was set up with purple flowers unmarred by the fires. And underneath stood a priest, beaming at us both.

I approached him cautiously. I was the reason for so much wrong in his country. He must hate me. But when we got near, he bowed to me deeply. "Empress."

"Thank you for doing this, Sai." Kohen embraced the man.

"It is my honor, my king."

My king. Somehow, in all of this, I'd forgotten Kohen was a king now.

How did a king and an empress come together as one?

I was about to find out because I didn't care about the repercussions of this wedding anymore. I wanted it for me, even if my people tried to take it from me.

The priest began by singing the most beautiful song in a

deep timbre in Imbrian. He belted to the sky, and I peered over at Kohen to find him staring at me with absolute adoration.

What did I do to deserve this kind of love?

Growing up under the harsh fist of my father, I never imagined any type of love. Jace was puppy love compared to this. Kohen was the other half of my soul.

The priest asked if we wanted to say anything to each other first, and Kohen reached up and stroked my cheek.

"Aisling, from this moment forward, I promise to love you with all that I am, to stand by your side through every high and low. I vow to cherish and respect you and hold you close in the hardest moments. I vow to lead our countries together as *one* and teach our children to do the same. But most of all, I vow to protect you, no matter what, forever and always."

Our countries as one. He wanted to join with Amersea again? Tears filled my eyes. Our children. My protection. It was so romantic, and my heart felt so full. I hadn't prepared for this. I had nothing planned, so I just spoke from my heart.

"Kohen, I never could have dreamed up a love like this. I promise you I am going to make mistakes."

He smiled.

"But I vow to always right my wrongs and respect your opinion, even though mine is probably better."

Both the priest and Kohen laughed.

"To lead our countries as one and to always come home to you. I love you."

The priest placed his hands over mine and Kohen's, joining them together. "It is my great pleasure to pronounce you husband and wife." He squeezed our hands and then bowed to us both before walking away.

"That was it?" I asked. "We're married?"

"According to Imbrian law. A priest has heard our love declared and sealed our bond. Now, he will write the declaration down and file it away in the hall of records. It's official, Aisling. You are my wife."

Official. I was officially Kohen's wife!

"Oh my stars, I'm married," I said, almost unable to believe it.

"Yes, wife, you are," he grinned.

I moaned, "Say it again." My heart ached to hear it a thousand times.

He grinned. "Wife." Leaning forward, he captured my mouth into a kiss and then pulled back, peering down at me. "Stay one night with me," he begged, "then we can figure all the hard stuff out in the morning."

I looked around at the half-burned-out building and then off to the side where a big white silk tent had been erected. I assumed that's where he meant for us to stay.

"Okay," I told him.

'I'll fly around the perimeter with Onyx,' Liana told me. I'd forgotten she was here somewhere.

'Thank you.'

'I'm happy for you, Aisling. No one should dictate who you love and marry, least of all duty.'

She was right. It was my life, my forever, and I wasn't going to spend it with anyone less than Kohen. My *husband.*

He led me over to the tent and unzipped it. I peered in and smiled. A thick bed with luscious blankets had been set up inside. We were in the middle of nowhere, and it couldn't be more perfect. The tent was large, over eight feet tall, so I could step in and not have to crouch. In the corner was a metal portable fireplace with logs already burning behind glass.

"This is really nice," I told him.

"Thanks. It's what our traders use when traveling long distances between villages. They pack everything on their mules or horses and live on the road."

I knew cars were a rarity in Imbria. They preferred the older modes of travel, like horseback.

I went to the corner, where a little washbasin sat with fresh water inside. The little rug at the end of the bed was a nice touch. It was homey, and for moment, I wanted to stay here forever with Kohen, never going back to reality and duty. Live in this tent, catch fish and deer, and cook on the fire stove. It would be a simple life. A nice life.

I peered down at the stunning ring on my hand. His mother's. When I looked up, I found him watching me.

"Your people will never forgive me." I shook my head. "And mine will never forgive you."

He walked across the room like a lion, long strides, eyes never leaving mine.

"And yet they do," he stated, leaning forward to kiss my collarbone, sending chills down my spine.

"You've seen it?" I asked.

He nodded, kissing a line across my neck and causing my knees to go weak.

"How? What do we do to convince them?"

He pulled back and met my gaze. "I have no idea. I try not to worry about the things I can't control."

His statement caused a giant weight to lift from my shoulders. Trying not to worry about things I couldn't control was something I'd never done before...

What if I tried that? At least for tonight?

Stepping forward, I took Kohen's face in my hands and kissed him hungrily. I kissed him how I'd always wanted to, without restraint, without care for who saw, who heard, who knew. He growled, and I pushed him onto the bed, falling on top of him.

"Kohen Badshah?" I sucked his bottom lip.

"Yes, Empress?" He panted into my ear.

"Show me one of the perks of being your wife," I taunted.

He smiled against my mouth and then grabbed my hips. One second, I was on top of him, and the next, he yanked me off, tossing me to the side, and then hovered over me. I laughed, but then, as I looked up, I gasped.

Stars. The ceiling of the tent was cut out and replaced with mesh netting, so I was looking up at the beautiful night sky. As Kohen slowly undressed me and we made love, I realized another one of his predictions had come true. We made love under a bed of stars, and I did indeed cry out his name.

CHAPTER
SEVENTEEN

Aisling

When the morning light filtered through the open tent roof, I smiled, looking up to find Kohen watching me sleep. I was draped over his bare chest, tangled in his arms.

"Good morning, my queen," he said.

Queen. Is that what I would become?

"Morning." I kissed him chastely before going over to the washbasin to brush my teeth and wash my face.

It was back to reality. I was already thinking of the Lottery and how to tell Elaine I married Kohen Badshah!

"Are you freaking out?" Kohen asked as he came up beside me.

"A little," I laughed, looking down at the ring on my finger. I had zero excitement when Alek gave me a ring, but every time I looked at this one, it gave me butterflies. Which reminded me I'd have to tell Alek.

"Regrets?" Kohen asked, hurt lacing through his voice.

I peered over at him, meeting his blue-eyed gaze. "No," I said firmly. "Just a lot of stuff to deal with. I think we should keep this quiet for now until I figure out how to tell everyone."

I pointed to the ring.

Kohen nodded, but was acting closed off. He brushed his teeth quietly, and then we stepped outside together, hands threaded through each other's.

I felt different after last night. Older somehow? I was a wife. How the hell had that happened?

"I have to tell you something," Kohen said beside me, and my stomach dropped out. That didn't sound good. He was acting off.

I faced him, and he took my face in his hands. "Remember when I told you there would be a time when your power wouldn't work?" he said.

I racked my memory and nodded. "You said I would need it, and it wouldn't come to me."

Kohen sighed. "When that happens, you are with Maxim."

Chills rose up my arms. "With Maxim, how?"

Kohen was silent for a moment. "As his wife."

A lump formed in my throat as my heart picked up speed in my chest. "Do you think it will still happen?" I asked him.

Now that he was seeing multiple futures, I hoped this one wasn't possible.

Kohen brushed the hair back from my face. "You are *my* wife. That won't change," he said, but his face betrayed his true answer. He wasn't sure what he thought anymore.

Liana landed with Onyx beside us, and I peered over at her.

'We should get back. The cadets are coming out of the Wilds.'

I nodded. Looking down at Kohen's mother's ring on my hand one last time, I pulled it off and slipped it onto the locket chain at my neck, the one with my mother's picture in it. Kohen watched me quietly, and I chewed on my lip.

"I'm going to call a truce between our people. Draft up some kind of long-term peace agreement or something we can both sign." Continuing to bomb each other now was just stupid.

Kohen nodded. "And when you are ready to tell them of our marriage, I will gladly sign Imbria back into Amersea. We can rule it as one. Together."

"You would do that?"

He nodded. "We are stronger together."

I didn't want to leave him. I wanted to drag him back into the tent and *never* leave. He seemed to be thinking the same thing.

"We can do this." Kohen grasped my fingers. "A short period of hardship for a lifetime of happiness."

He pulled me into his arms and kissed me as I smiled against his mouth. "You are like a ball of sunshine sometimes," I told him.

"And you are like a rain cloud sometimes."

I laughed as he kissed my neck.

"I'll miss you. Please don't stay away too long," he begged.

I ran my fingers through his hair, but my mind was on what he'd said about marrying Maxim and not having my power, about Valor getting killed or Victory getting kidnapped.

"Kohen, what if all that bad stuff in your visions comes true?" Because there is nothing I would not do to protect my sisters.

He brushed his finger over my lips. "Don't worry, I will always protect you."

"I'm not worried about me. I'm worried about my sisters. My people."

"I will protect them, too," he declared.

"That's valiant, Kohen, but how can you possibly? Your powers are great, but Maxim's might be greater. You cannot come at an entire army with fire and future sight."

He gave me a cocky grin then. "Yes, I can." There was an all-knowing smile on his lips.

"What are you talking about?"

He eyed the tent and then Liana and Onyx. "I wasn't ready to show you this yet. It's still a prototype."

Then he dipped into the tent and came out with a small wooden box.

My brows drew together. "What's that?"

Kohen peered up at me. "This is what our future children's children will fight wars with. I saw it in a vision from a time when I'm not even alive anymore."

"What?" I asked, shocked. "How is that possible?"

He shook his head, unlocking the latch on the box to reveal a...

"What's it called?" I asked as he gripped the steel base of the object.

"A gun," he told me, and for some reason, chills raced down my spine.

"What does it do?" I stepped closer, inspecting it. It was a huge L-shaped hunk of metal, but the point of it was a barrel with an opening. There were tiny metal cylinders in the box that Kohen loaded into the back of the... gun.

"It shoots projectiles out. Like an arrow launcher but smaller, more deadly, with the force of a train. Like a cannon you can hold in your hand."

I gasped.

"I'm still working on aiming, but here... stand behind me and watch." He held both arms out before him, gripping the weapon with his finger on a little lever. Then he aimed at the remaining brick wall of the burned-down house.

"Plug your ears," he told me.

"Why?" I asked.

"Trust me," he said.

I did, and then a foreign sound ripped past my ears, like something had cracked open and echoed throughout the canyon. Even the force of it reverberated through my chest. I gasped as a small puff of smoke curled up from the back of the weapon.

"What did it do?" I asked, looking around for some damage.

"It was too fast for you to track since you didn't know what to look for. Come here." He stowed the weapon at his hip and then walked me over to the wall. When I saw a perfect hole punched through the brick, I gasped.

"It went through brick?" An arrow couldn't do that.

Kohen nodded. "Imagine what it could do to an enemy's heart..."

It was an unsettling thought. I'd never seen such an incredible weapon before.

"How many of these do you have?"

"Just one. I've been working with my blacksmith for two months, perfecting it. I got the vision the night you found out... the truth," he said wearily.

If we had a hundred of these, we could take Luska in one night.

"Can you make more?"

"With time."

I nodded, smiling. "Good. I should go. I have a thousand things to do and—"

His lips were on mine in an instant, and I melted into his touch. It reminded me of last night and the pleasure I'd felt, the way he'd tenderly made love to me and called me *wife* any chance he got.

"Everything will be okay," he whispered into my ear before stepping back.

It should have felt like a promise, but instead, it felt like a consolation. Like he was warning me of a storm coming and to take cover.

CHAPTER
EIGHTEEN

isling

I WAS on a happy high from my night with Kohen, hardly able to believe I'd just become his wife in secret. But nothing had felt more right. I didn't deserve his forgiveness after everything I'd done, everything my father had done—to him and his people. But he gave it, and not just that— he bound himself to me for eternity.

'I'm happy for you,' Liana said again.

I smiled, the wind whipping against my face. *'Thank you. I'm sorry I didn't listen when you tried to tell me my father was a bad person,'* I told her.

Reaching up, I touched the necklace at my throat with a

smile, fingering the ring there. I had no idea how this would work when I could tell people, but... being Kohen's wife, having peace between our nations. It was the only way I could stay true to myself.

'Land at the front gates of the Wilds. I want to check in,' I told her.

My mind was running wild, trying to keep all the things in line that had to be done. I had cadets in the Wilds, I had the training center ready to start up another boot camp, I had my sisters to protect, the peace treaty with Imbria to draft, and Luska to keep an eye on, especially after we tore down part of the Wall. It felt like too many moving pieces.

When Liana began to descend over the gates, I saw there were already dozens of cadets with creatures outside, getting triaged in the medical tent. Hopefully for minor injuries.

It was the morning of the third day. Most should be making it out by now. I'd expected more than this. Maybe they'd already been bused back to the capital.

'Look up,' Liana told me.

I snapped my head up and gasped.

At first I pulled for my magic, thinking what I was seeing was a Luskin assault. But when I recognized Charlene, I grinned.

Charlene and over three dozen others were riding Talanagi.

"Empress!" Charlene screamed over the wind. She rode a black-feathered griffin with blue ember marks. She had a large claw mark gash on her left arm and was covered in dirt.

I laughed in shock as the troop of cadets flew around me

in circles. Dragons, winged lions, griffins, so many flying Talanagi. It was incredible.

Our plan had worked. We now had a force to properly fight Luska with.

I flew in circles with the other cadets, who were whooping and yelling into the sky with excitement and joy lifted in my chest. Things were looking up. This peace that Valor spoke about, that she thought might be impossible in her lifetime, seemed just within reach to me now.

After checking in with the guards at the gate and congratulating the cadets who had made it out, I flew home.

By the time I got home in the late morning, the girls and Elaine had already left to head back to Sky Reach.

"You just missed them," Tetra told me as she stroked Ariyel's fur. They were both curled on the couch. "I told them you were checking in at the Wilds."

Dang. I hadn't meant to be gone so long. "I'll see them tonight. And I *was* checking in at the Wilds," I told her.

She grinned devilishly. "You look different."

I smiled, trying not to. "What are you talking about? No, I don't."

I couldn't stop smiling.

"Aisling Everhart, you're madly in love. Tell me everything. What did Kohen say?"

If I couldn't trust my best friend, who could I trust? I sat down next to her.

Pulling out my necklace, I slid the ring off and slipped it onto my ring finger.

She gasped. "You're engaged to Kohen! You went to apologize for your dad pinning a terrorist attack on his father and killing him... and you got engaged?"

I shook my head, and her face fell in confusion.

"I kind of actually married him?"

"WHAT!" she shrieked, and I laughed.

"It was like a spur-of-the-moment thing. But it feels so right."

"Aisling, that is *so* unlike you. I'm loving this rebellious empress." She pulled the ring closer and looked at it. "It's beautiful."

"It was his mother's," I told her. "We had the best night. He had a priest waiting there, and it was... perfect. Just us two."

Tetra pouted. "I mean, I'm kinda mad you didn't wait for me. Can we have a big party to celebrate or something?"

My face fell. "I don't know when we can actually tell people about this, Tetra. Amersea thinks Kohen's dad caused the Great Blackout and that he killed my father. I can't tell them I've married him."

"Then tell them your dad did it and clear the Badshah name and all of the hate against Imbrians."

Her plea tore at my heart. "Then they will think I come from bad stock, and the Everhart name will be tarnished." But even as I said it, I felt selfish.

Tetra frowned. "Well, you at least have to tell the admirals. You can't let them go on thinking Imbria is our enemy, or that Kohen is. Not if you love him, you won't."

Her last sentence stung as if she was judging me for not calling an emergency meeting right now to clear Kohen's name with the higher military officials.

"Okay, you're right. I will. Geeze," I told her, shame coloring my cheeks.

"Sorry, I just... feel bad that this entire time we've judged Imbria for something they never did."

I did, too. I actually felt sick about it if I focused on it too long. "You're right, though. I shouldn't care about my family name more than I should care about the truth."

She pulled me into a side hug. "This is hard stuff. Be gentle with yourself."

I nodded. Tetra was the best. So understanding and supportive. Even if I was scared of the outcome, I had to do what was right.

"Did you have sex?" she asked casually, and I pulled away from her, laughing.

"What? You're married. You totally had sex! What's it like? Was it good? Did it hurt?" Her rapid-fire questions caused my cheeks to go hot. I really needed to call a meeting with the admirals, but ten more minutes with my bestie wouldn't matter, right?

Tetra's face fell then as if she'd just realized something.

"What?" I asked.

"What are you going to tell Alek?"

Oh crap. Out of everything that happened the last twenty-four hours, I'd forgotten about sweet Alek.

CHAPTER NINETEEN

Aisling

Nerves ate a hole in my stomach as I stood on Alek's doorstep and knocked. He'd still be in town from the Lottery. We weren't called to be back in Sky Reach until tomorrow.

When he answered, he grinned hugely. "Aisling. Come in." He opened the door wider, and his mother scurried from the couch to stand. "Empress." She fumbled with a curtsy, and I hated myself for what I was about to do.

I shook my head. "Sorry. I need to talk to you privately, actually." I waved to his mom.

Alek stepped outside, looking expectantly at me as he shut the door behind him. "What's up?"

My heart leaped into my throat. I hated this. I hated that he was such a great guy.

"You're amazing," I said, unable to keep the tears from my eyes and the emotion from clogging my throat.

His face fell.

"But...?"

My chest heaved. I didn't want this to break him like Jace broke me. "But I can't marry you." I pulled the small ring from my pocket and handed it to him.

He froze, not taking it.

"Why? I thought we had an agreement. For the future of Amersea."

If anyone deserved the truth, it was Alek.

"We did. But I have selfishly decided to follow my heart and put my wants before that of my country."

He looked down at me. "Kohen?"

I nodded.

He yanked the ring from my fingers. "Aisling, he killed your father. He killed *you*. Have you lost your mind?"

I sighed. "Listen, this is beyond classified, but I feel you deserve the truth. If you were to tell anyone, my life could be in danger."

He appeared concerned, then and nodded. "I'd never do anything to put you in danger, Aisling."

He was so sweet. I hoped he found someone good to erase all the damage I was no doubt doing right now. "I have evidence that my father was the one who caused the Great Blackout. He pinned it on Ravi Badshah on purpose to take over their land."

Alek gasped. "Holy crap."

I nodded. "Kohen was protecting me. My father was behind the attacks on me at boot camp." I knew that now. Even without the evidence, it was there all along.

"I don't even know what to say," he said.

"Say you're happy for me, that you'll support me, and we'll stay friends."

He smiled sadly then, slipping the ring into his pocket. "If you're happy, I'm happy, Aisling."

His comment broke my heart just a little bit more, and I pulled him in for a tight hug. "One day, you'll find a woman who deserves you."

He squeezed me back, inhaling as if remembering my scent for the last time.

We pulled apart, and I walked away without another word.

I had to call a meeting and clear Kohen's family name. If it was the only thing I did, it would be worth it.

Over the next hour, I told the admirals the truth about the night of the blackout. Most of them were in Riverine, and it was easy to call the meeting at my father's house. I produced the safe with all the papers and maps. They were in shock and disbelief, trying to make a case for how this could be anything else, but ultimately, the note in his handwriting sealed their decision.

We can call it the Great Blackout. Blame Imbria. Kill Badshah. Take over. Double our land.

Those few sentences caused an uproar within the meeting room.

Commander Ledger slammed a fist on the table. "That bastard!"

"I can't believe it," Admiral Caruso said.

"I want you to question everyone in this room and make sure they weren't party to it," I told her in front of the ten people present.

There was a minor outroar at that, but in the end, they relented, saying they understood. If my father had help, I wanted that person out of our leadership.

"Draft a peace treaty with Imbria. They will join us again. We will become one nation."

Commander Ledger's brows bunched together. "How can you be so sure? Especially if they get wind of this? They'll want your head on a stick."

"Kohen Badshah will sign it. Trust me," I said. "We need to be united now more than ever before. After the recent Riverine attack from Luska, and tearing down the Wall, we have no idea what they will do next."

Commander Ledger shook his head. "Hang on, Empress. It's our job to advise you on what's best for your safety and our country. We cannot draft a reunification with Imbria on a, '*trust me*'. We've burned half their country. If Kohen Badshah has told you he will join us again and sign a peace treaty, it could be a trap."

"It's not a trap," I said.

"How can you be sure?" Admiral Caruso said.

"Yeah, just because young Badshah might have agreed to a peace treaty verbally doesn't mean he'll sign," Admiral Blade echoed.

"He'll sign it!" I shouted.

"But how are you sure?" Commander Ledger asked.

"Because I married him last night!" I screamed, and the entire room went silent.

Crap. I hadn't intended for that to get out.

"You wouldn't dare," Blade said in disbelief.

"Why not? He, his family, his country—they are not the enemy. My father was!"

More silence.

"The people won't accept this," Caruso said. "This doesn't leave the room."

The next hour was spent convincing them I had, in fact, married Kohen Badshah and that a priest was present and it was legally binding. They went into "damage control," as if I was some angry teen who had gone off and done something rash.

Had I? Maybe. But it felt like the best decision I ever made.

I showed them the ring, and half the men in the room rolled their eyes. "Don't wear that in public. Tell no one," Admiral Blade said.

Why was everyone treating this like some big mistake? I guess prejudices didn't die right away, even with evidence that you were wrong. Maybe they had to slowly be starved of oxygen and fade away. It would take time.

"What if the people did accept it? What if this is what finally brings our two countries together? Like actually together as equals. Not like last time when they were seen as beneath us. Not as a conquered nation. This would be a mutual merging of two nations. Stronger together."

Commander Ledger hung his head into his hands, and rubbed his temples, and then looked up into my eyes. It was like looking at an older Jace. "The people aren't ready for this. You tell them you married Kohen Badshah, and they will have you hanging from a tree in Emberlane Park by nightfall."

"He's right," Admiral Caruso said.

My heart fell. "But we have evidence of what my father did."

Blade nodded. "We also have a confession that Badshah killed your father and then killed you. Even if it was to retaliate for what your father did to his. People won't see him in a good light. He's still a killer."

They were right. How did you overcome years of prejudice and smear campaigns? They would hold anything they could against Kohen, against his people. Even armed with the truth. The very men and women in this room were doing it. They were still judging Kohen on his past, on rumors, on where he was from.

"He didn't kill my father to retaliate. He did it to protect me. My father was also behind the attack on my life at boot camp," I declared. Might as well just let the whole truth out there, at least with everyone in this room.

Gasps, more shocked expressions.

I opened my mouth to say more when Liana burst into my mind with frantic energy. *'Get outside. Zara is here without Valor.'*

It felt like the entire room spun as I bolted up from my chair, muttering something about my sister's creature being outside, and then I ran. Down the hall, past the kitchen, and out the front door, I burst into the yard of my father's palatial mansion and skidded to a halt when I saw Zara, bloody gashes all along her left side, her right wing burned slightly.

'Luskins took Victory on our way to Sky Reach,' she rambled into my mind. *'Elaine fought with all she had but will die without help. Vespa died. Valor and Virtue are safe and hiding in the woods where I left them.'*

A sob, which turned into an angry roar, ripped from my throat.

Admiral Caruso burst outside behind me. "What's wrong?"

I felt out of my body, unsure how I got from where I was standing to Liana's back.

"Luska took Victory. Vespa is dead. Elaine is dying," I managed to say before Liana took off after Zara, who was leading the way.

Vespa was the first creature who'd ever let me touch her. I'd grown up as a young child with her in my bed every night as Elaine put me to sleep.

'You're sure Vespa is gone, not just injured?' I managed to ask Zara, finding I could speak to her as easily as I could with Liana.

'I'm sure. She's... dead,' was all she said.

'Did they hurt Victory? Did they leave demands?' So much rushed through my head. Kohen saying he saw a future where Victory had been taken. Elaine being hurt and wondering if Valor could heal her.

'Victory was unhurt when I last saw her. They left a letter.'

Stars, I felt sick—my sweet little sister carted off into Luska. Would they torture her? Of course they would. She might be fourteen, but she was an Everhart. The sick feeling became too much, and I leaned over Liana and vomited into the sky.

'They might not have plans to harm her. Wait until you read the letter,' Liana told me.

It was good advice, but I couldn't calm my mind. I was already mentally living in a terrible future without Vespa, Elaine, or Victory.

It took a nerve-racking two hours of flying before we got close to my sisters. Zara was a fast flyer, but not as fast as Liana, and we had to follow her. She couldn't explain where in the woods they were hiding, but she remembered how to get there.

When we stumbled upon our family car, flipped over on the road, and smoking, I gasped. There was blood... tire marks—so much blood.

Six bodies. I counted six bodies. Dizziness washed over me as I identified our driver, Verik.

'Sorry. Your driver lost his life fighting. I forgot to tell you. The others are Luskin. Elaine killed them.'

Verik. He'd been our driver for as long as I could remember.

I peered over at her. *'It's okay, you've been through a lot. You did the right thing hiding the girls and Elaine in the woods and then getting me.'*

I could see the pain in her eyes. She was hurting because Valor was hurting. Valor, a triplet who had scarcely ever been without her sister, had just witnessed a live kidnapping, and her mother figure was near death.

I realized I hadn't thought enough to stop and get a med-kit, and prayed that Elaine was still alive. I couldn't go through Victory being kidnapped and mourning Elaine's death at the same time. It would end me.

I glanced back at the five bodies. Elaine was a badass fighter; she taught me everything I knew. They must have had over a dozen soldiers to overpower her.

I clutched the ring that hung from my necklace, the one Kohen had given me, and wished he were here. I needed a hug. I needed him to hold me and tell me everything was going to be okay. I was spiraling out of control.

If Maxim laid a single finger on my sister, I'd burn the entire world down.

'As will I,' Liana agreed.

Okay, breathe. Just take it one step at a time. I told myself as I fought off a panic. I wanted to blindly fly to Luska and look for my sister, but I had to take this one step at a time.

Step one: make sure Elaine was still alive.

Step two: read the letter Maxim left for me.

Step three: get my sister back at any cost.

I scanned the space frantically as we began to descend into an open clearing.

'She said they are hidden in thick trees. We have to walk from here,' Liana told me. We were feet from the ground when Liana cocked her head to the side.

'Onyx and Kohen are on their way, too.'

Relief rushed through me at that. I needed someone to mentally process all of this with. He must have had a vision and was now on his way to help.

The second Liana hit the ground and Zara pointed in the direction of where my sisters and Elaine were, I took off running.

"Valor!" I bellowed, pulling my sword. "Virtue!"

"Aisling!" one of my sisters sobbed. Her voice was so distorted I couldn't tell if it was Valor or Virtue. My heart beat madly as I leaped over fallen trees and ferns to find the girls. I skidded to a stop when I saw them. Elaine was sprawled out in Valor's lap. Tears were streaming down her face as she held her hands over blood-encrusted wounds on Elaine's body, plugging holes in our governess with her fingers. Virtue was beside them, hugging her knees and staring off into the forest.

"I can't fix it," Valor said. "I can't see it. The picture isn't clear, not like with Tetra... I can't..." Valor mumbled.

She was in shock. They both were. There was so much blood. I sheathed my sword and kneeled down, placing my fingers over Elaine's neck. She was so pale; there was a very faint pulse, and her chest was barely rising. Off to the side was a letter with bloody fingerprints and my name on the front.

"Vespa died," Virtue sobbed. "Right in front of us."

I felt out-of-body. I had to wall up every emotion and turn into a machine. Otherwise, nothing would get done.

"That's okay. Elaine's alive," I said brightly, trying to put some life into my voice.

Virtue and Valor's head snapped to look at me for the first time.

"She is?" Valor said. "I wasn't sure."

I nodded. "You did so good."

I began ripping strips off my shirt as I triaged the situation. Some kind of bolt shooter had been used. I could tell by how big the puncture wounds were, but there were gashes, too, like that of a creature. And burn marks.

Oh stars, it was bad.

I peeled Valor's hands one at a time, shoving balls of linen cloth in the holes to stop the bleeding and then tying tight strips over it.

"You did so good, Valor," I praised her again.

"Don't lie!" she screamed, still hysterical. "I'm a healer, and I can't heal her. Elaine..." The way she said her name caused a lump to form in my throat.

Virtue said what we were all thinking: "Mom..."

To these girls, who never met the mother who birthed us, *she* was their mother.

I couldn't lose it. Not here in front of them, but tears were clouding my vision, so I blinked them back. "We don't know how your gift works yet, Val. You need time and training. You did great. Can you go take Virtue to the creek over there, wash your hands, and bring me some water? There is a canteen in Liana's saddlebag."

Part of my training included shock. Getting the person to focus on a task away from the trauma was best.

Valor nodded, gently moving Elaine's head as she stood.

"I don't want to leave her," Virtue whined.

"We're just going to wash our hands and get water," Valor said. She sounded more alert and calm. Giving her the task was a good idea. They were both covered in blood. I had no doubt they'd witnessed a gruesome scene. Elaine had killed five Luskin soldiers, protecting them. I couldn't imagine how many they sent to overwhelm her, Vespa, and Verik. A dozen? I didn't want to ask; my sisters had finally started to focus on something else.

'They tried to take all three girls and leave a message with Elaine,' Zara told me. *'A dozen in total. Four had flying Talanagi with baskets to drop the rest. I helped Elaine as much as I could with the flying ones, but... there were just so many.'*

'You did great,' I assured her as I plugged hole after hole in the body of the woman who'd raised me.

Leaning forward, I whispered in her ear. "Don't you die on me. I need you." I had to get her stable enough that she would survive a flight to Sky Reach, where we had a surgeon. One jerky move, and she could bleed out.

Liana cocked her head to the side. *'Kohen is meeting resistance with the Fleet. They've spotted him.'*

My eyes widened. If they shot him down, this would really be the worst day of my life. *'Can you go up there and settle things down? I can't leave Elaine.'*

She nodded.

'I will go, too, and speak to their minds,' Zara said.

That was a big help.

'Thank you,' I told them.

I'd barely had time to tell the admirals to draft up a peace treaty with Luska. If my Fleet saw Kohen flying here, they would shoot him down.

I couldn't worry about that right now. There was so much blood, and even with my aggressively packing holes in Elaine, which had to hurt, she wasn't even flinching.

Stars, don't take her from me, I begged.

"We got the water." Valor handed it out to me. I hadn't even heard her approach.

I took it, taking a swig, even though I didn't need it, and peered at my sisters. They were wet but mostly clean of blood on their skin. Their clothes were another matter.

"Remember the story Elaine used to tell you when you were really little? The one with the bunny and the horse?" I asked the girls. "Tell it to me. I need something else to focus on," I said while I watched the plugs I'd created in Elaine's body for any leaks. Like she was a car leaking oil and not precious lifeblood.

Valor seemed to know what I was doing. Trying to keep things calm, she told the story.

It was a silly story about a friendship between a bunny and a horse, and how the bunny and horse fought over carrots on the farm they lived at until they teamed up and stole all of the carrots and made the farmer mad. It was a cute story that took about ten minutes to tell.

When she finished, I heard the thumping of feet behind me, and I craned my neck to see Kohen, his two brothers, and a stranger I didn't know. He was a tall Imbrian man with a small fox creature that reminded me of Vespa. Liana, Zara, and the other two dragons, who belonged to Arjun and Tej, walked through the forest behind them.

I had no words for Kohen. I didn't even know what to say. My hands were encrusted with drying blood from Elaine, and one of my sisters was gone. There was a hole in my heart the size of Amersea.

"Please save her," Kohen asked the Imbrian man in his forties with the fox creature.

"Yes, my king." The man nodded, walking over to kneel at my feet.

"Are you a surgeon? If she can travel, we have supplies at the army base," I asked him.

"No, Empress, I'm not a surgeon. I'm a healer. I need you to step away so your energy doesn't influence the situation," he said kindly but firmly.

I stood, hands shaking, as I stepped away from Elaine.

'His energy is pure and kind-hearted, but he is sad. He's seen a lot of death,' Liana told me.

Hopefully not because he wasn't a good healer.

I watched as he scanned his hands over Elaine's body, grimacing as he did. His fox creature walked up and down the side of Elaine's body, sniffing as she went. The irony that Elaine had lost Vespa, her fox, only to hopefully be healed by a man with a fox creature was not lost on me.

The man began to hum, a pretty rhythmic sound, and I watched in fascination as small threads of white silver light left his fingers and went into Elaine's body. I glanced over at

Valor to see if she could see it too, and her jaw was dropped open. Everyone's was. It looked like his gift was similar to hers, and thank the stars for that.

'He's also using sound to help heal,' Liana told me as she watched the man curiously.

I didn't know what that meant. I didn't care, so long as it meant Elaine would survive.

Kohen picked up the white letter from the ground and approached me, pulling me off to the side to speak privately. His voice filled with compassion. "This will take a while. He works slowly, but he's the best healer we have."

I nodded, taking the letter, knowing I had to not only worry about Elaine but also Victory.

Whatever was in this letter would be some type of ransom or demand for her, and I had to deal with that.

"Do you want my brothers to fly your sisters to Sorak and keep them safe?" Kohen asked, pulling me from my thoughts. "No one will look for them there."

Take them out of Amersea? I hadn't even thought about that.

I met his eyes and saw so much compassion there. But something else, too, something that scared me.

Sadness.

Why was he sad? What did he know?

"Did you see her die, Kohen?" I asked. "Just tell me."

He shook his head. "I think she makes it out. I've seen her in future visions."

I frowned. "Then why do you look so sad?"

He gestured to the letter in my hands. "Why don't you

read that? Let's focus on Victory. I'm going to have my brothers take your sisters to Sorak, okay? I think that's best."

He was treating me a bit like I couldn't think for myself, and I was starting to wonder if I couldn't. Was I in shock? I felt frozen, and it honestly was a relief to have someone to lean on who could make decisions right now.

Why hadn't I read the letter yet? Why didn't I tear it open and start barking orders and rallying the troops to get my sister back?

"Okay," I said, trying to fight through the grief and panic that were clawing their way inside my body.

I told my sisters to go with Arjun and Tej and that Elaine was going to be fine. They happily obliged. It seemed like they would do anything to get out of here. Virtue sat behind Valor on Zara, and they left. Seeing the three dragons fly off into the sky made me question if I was making a mistake.

"Won't your people hurt them if they find out who they are?" I asked.

Kohen looked offended. "My people don't have the same prejudices as yours."

Ouch.

But he was right. Maybe his people were more forgiving and accepting than mine. Maybe they saw my sisters as separate from my father and me. I hoped so. Because Imbria might be the only safe place for them now.

I looked up at Kohen and then at the letter. "I'm scared to open it."

What if it said they killed her? What if it said they stuck

her head on a spike on the Wall? I felt paralyzed at the thought.

Kohen peered over his shoulder at the healer, who was still humming and waving his hands over Elaine, weaving silver strings up and down her body.

Kohen pulled me aside even farther so that the tree was mostly blocking us, and then he took me into his arms. When the weight of his body crushed against me, I finally let myself relax. The buzzing shock that had me frozen this whole time melted into pure panic and grief.

"Elaine is like my mother," I whispered against his neck.

"I know." He rubbed small circles on my back.

"And Victory, she's the sweetest of all of them. This will change her forever, even if I get her back."

"You'll get her back," he said confidently, and I pulled back, my heart lifting for the first time in days.

"Have you seen that?"

His face fell. "I don't know anymore. Everything is so... converged."

I frowned. "Converged?"

"I don't know which path leads to what anymore, but I do know that I will never let anything bad happen to you, okay?" He took my face in his hands. "No matter what that letter says, no matter what you have to do, you'll always be *my* wife."

You'll always be my wife.

At that moment, I was sure that Kohen did know something awful, and he just didn't want to tell me. Maybe it was better that way.

"Let me clean up real fast," I told him and walked over to the creek, plunging my hands into the cool water and scrubbing off Elaine's blood. As the creek ran red, I steeled myself to open the letter. When I was done, I walked back over to Kohen, who patiently waited for me, and then, without wasting another second, I ripped the letter open.

Beloved Aisling,

I've decided I'm done playing games. You deprived me of my sister, so now I'm taking yours. Come to Luska and become my wife, and I'll keep her alive. Surrender your country to me and join our lands, and there will be peace. If you do not immediately do this, I'll skin your sister alive and drop the biggest bomb you've ever seen on Riverine. I will have Amersea either by force or marriage. Your choice.

Maxim

I looked over at Kohen, who had been reading over my shoulder, and though his jaw muscle was ticcing, he didn't look too surprised. I remembered then something he had said. *It ends with you married to Maxim.*

"Was it always going to end like this? Me with Maxim? Is that how Virtue and my people stay safe?"

Kohen's fists clenched. He looked tortured by whatever visions he must have seen.

"Kohen, just tell me what you've seen. I can handle it. I'm a big girl." Though my heart was breaking at the idea of surrendering to Maxim, signing over my lands and my body to him—forever—I would do it in a second to save my sister.

Kohen's voice was hollow. "I've seen many outcomes. In some, Amersea is a crater with no life. In others, it thrives."

It was hard to hear, but I had to. "In the one where it thrives?"

Kohen sighed. "You marry Maxim. I don't know for how long, but there is a wedding." He sounded so pained that I knew this must be tearing him apart.

"And if we fight? Rally our army and storm the wall?"

Kohen swallowed hard. "Virtue dies, and Maxim makes good on the bomb threat. It's like nothing we've ever seen. Riverine is no longer on maps in the future after that."

I gasped at his comment. No longer on maps! How big was this bomb?

"So I have to marry him?" I felt like a child with the way my voice cracked. "That's the only way?"

Kohen looked like he was going to explode with rage and punch a tree, but he just gritted his jaw, chest heaving. "Right now, they have every flying creature in their army in the sky. If you try to sneak even one assassin in, they kill Victory. If you try to kill Maxim before the wedding, they kill Victory. Aisling, I've seen a dozen scenarios, and as much as it pains me to say this... you... have to marry him."

Tears filled my eyes. Having my will taken from me, which is exactly what this was, was my worst nightmare. That's why I didn't like using my power on others. I would hate for the same to be done to me.

Kohen leaned his head against my forehead. "Just know

that it won't be real. Because we married first, it won't be legitimate."

That didn't mean I wanted to do it. A tear slipped down my cheek, and Kohen grasped my chin, tilting my face up to meet his eyes. "I won't let him hurt you or Victory, do you understand?"

"You can't say that," I told him.

He grasped my chin a little tighter, lacing a finality in his words. "I. Won't. Let. You. Be. Harmed," he growled out.

I believed that *he* believed that, that he would probably get himself killed trying to plan some big rescue mission.

"Okay," I said to make him feel better. "But I need to ask you a favor, one that I have no business asking after what I put your people through. After what my father put your people through..."

"If you want something from me, Aisling, my answer is always yes."

I laughed, but it turned into a weird sob. They spoke about love like ours in romance books. But in those, they had happy endings, and in mine... I ended up with Maxim and my sister was a prisoner. I'd only ever really had Kohen for one night. That's all we got.

I swallowed hard.

"What is your request, my love?" Kohen asked, brushing his finger over my bottom lip, sending tendrils of warmth down my spine.

"Take my people. Protect them? Please. I'll order a mass evacuation. That way, if Maxim hurts Victory and I get triggered and rip his throat out, and then he makes good on his threat... no one will die."

Kohen didn't falter even for a second. "Absolutely. Your people, your sisters, Elaine, they will be safe in Imbria."

"I don't deserve you. I never did." The way I treated him from day one, it made me sick to think about. And all the while, my father was the one who made their life hell and steal their land and enslave their people. It was wrong, and I didn't even know how to go about making it right.

"We deserve each other." He pulled my chin forward and kissed my mouth.

"Is there even any place left to send my people? I've burned half your country and bombed so many villages," I said distraughtly.

Kohen nodded. "You have, but my country is bigger than I think you ever thought it was. Sorak is fine, and our great capital Nimra, as well. Anything east of the open plains is thriving and we are rebuilding. My men are signing up for the reserve army, and we will be okay. There's room for everyone. They will need to bring tents and help farm, but there's room."

There's room. He wasn't saying no. He was saying he would make room, and I realized at that moment another prophecy he'd spoken had come true.

One day, you'll beg me to protect you. Except it wasn't me, it was everyone I cared about and had pledged to protect.

"Thank you." I didn't know what to say now. The letter indicated that I should leave now. That I stop at nothing to reach Maxim and just sign over my country and my life. "I need to write a letter to my admirals and to Valor," I told him.

He nodded and pulled a pen and paper from his pack.

Crouching down, I wrote a letter to the admirals telling them what I had to do in order to keep Victory alive and to keep Riverine from being wiped off the map. I told them to order a mass evacuation to Imbria and that Maxim had a huge bomb.

Then I wrote a letter to Valor, one that broke my heart.

Finally, I reached up to my neck and unclasped the locket that held my mother's picture and my wedding ring from Kohen. "Give this to Valor one day," I told him, clasping it around his neck and tucking it into his shirt as I tried to fight the emotions threatening to take hold of me.

His bottom lip shook as he met my gaze. "You'll give it to her yourself. We will find a way out of this. I just have to see a vision that shows me the steps to take."

I cupped my hand to his face and stroked his cheek. "Sometimes there's nothing you can do. Sometimes, you make your bed, and you have to lie in it."

I killed Maxim's sister. The reckoning of that day had come. "My admirals know we married. They know the truth about what my father did, and that yours was innocent. If you go to them with this letter, they will follow my orders."

"I hate this," he breathed.

I nodded. "Not more than I do." My voice cracked.

I peered over at the healer. He was still working over Elaine, and I had no idea if she would make it.

"Please take care of her," I told him.

"You know I will. I'll take care of everyone, Aisling—and you. Please trust me. I'll find a way to kill this bastard. I don't know why, but when you marry him, all of the visions I have make him seem untouchable. I have to find out why, and then I'll save you and Victory."

Untouchable. *Great.*

I turned around then because I sensed her.

Liana.

'I don't want to argue. I know you hate Maxim, but it's for Victory,' I told her.

She nodded. *'I'll fly you, though I doubt he will let me stay.'*

She understood, of course she did. I grasped her neck, hugging her tightly, and then turned to face Kohen, who stood like a stone, eyes wide.

"I'll figure this out," he said, as if in a dream. "I just need to have a vision that shows me the way."

I nodded, "Okay," I told him because now he needed my comfort.

"Don't lose hope. I'll come for you," he said.

"Okay," I repeated, lying through my teeth and clinging to him once more.

I needed to get out of here. I needed to get to Victory and make sure she wasn't hurt.

"Kohen, get my people out of here. If Maxim has hurt my sister, I'll rip his throat out with my teeth, and then he'll level Amersea."

Fear flashed across Kohen's face as if that was exactly what he was afraid of. "I will. I'll get everyone out, but it will take a few days. You have to keep the peace until then."

Keep the peace? That bastard had my sister.

"No promises," I told him. "And if your visions are wrong and I do have access to my power around him, I'll make him cut his own throat," I growled.

Kohen just stayed silent as if he knew that wasn't possible.

I didn't care. I'd reached the angry portion of this reality.

The woman whom we loved as a mother was on her deathbed, my innocent sister had been brutally kidnapped, and I was being forced into an arranged marriage.

All at the hands of Maxim Vlek.

If there was a way, I would make this bastard pay.

I slipped my leg onto Liana and peered at Kohen one last time. "I'm grateful for the time we had." My throat pinched with emotion. "For as long as I live, I'll wish we had more. Thank you for being gracious to me and my people. Goodbye, Kohen."

Liana kicked off the ground, and Kohen fell to his knees, punching the earth and screaming into the sky.

It was the cry of a broken man, helpless to do anything for a woman he loved. At that moment, I accepted my fate. I knew he was so distraught because he'd probably seen a hundred different versions of this play out, each one keeping me from him.

But that's how life was sometimes. Sometimes we had to make do with the cards we were dealt and not the ones we wanted.

CHAPTER
TWENTY

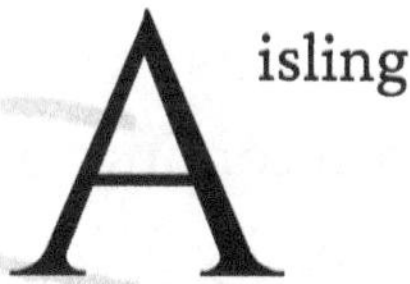

Aisling

As I flew over the wall, I saw my men stationed there peer up at me in confusion, waving their arms as if to tell me to stop. But I pressed on, ignoring their cries.

I had to hope that Kohen would be able to somehow evacuate my people. That Elaine would live. That my sisters would be okay. That the admirals and my people would obey my command. It was for their own good. I knew not all would choose to leave their homes and go to Imbria, but I hoped Kohen could be convincing enough to save as many as he could.

The right side of the wall was in a crumbled heap of stone.

'They're everywhere,' Liana breathed.

I peered up to see what she was talking about and gasped. Small dots in the sky, riders of flying Talanagi, were positioned every hundred feet or so across the Luskin sky. They held spears, bolt shooters, and swords, and they all looked my way, tracking Liana and me as if they were expecting me.

Kohen was right. Maxim had been planning this. There was no way out.

'I feel like I've failed you,' Liana said as she flew past a male rider on a black-feathered griffin. He allowed me to fly past without a flinch. They'd clearly been given instructions.

'I feel like I've failed myself,' I said. We were both coming to terms with the fact that I was doing this. I was literally flying into enemy territory to marry an evil man against my will.

'You could never fail me. I know it will be hard, but I want you to drop me off at the capital and then fly back to help Kohen. If Maxim allows it...'

'I don't know if I can leave you,' she admitted.

I nodded, my heart pinching. *'I know, but I have to think of my sister. She's terrified and alone. I have to also think of my people. Kohen will need your help. You will be of no help to me. Maxim will make sure of that.'*

We passed another rider just hovering in the air, giving me a smug look as I passed.

'This reminds me of the Great Fall,' she said, and I bristled. She never spoke of it, but maybe now she was ready.

'How so?' I pried a little, ready to respect her if she went quiet or changed the subject.

'My grandmother found her mate, a firebird from a less respected tribe. He had a humble family name and was not seen as powerful, but she loved him—she chose him.'

My heart pinched at her words.

'We mate for life. Once you choose, that is it. The bond is forever. But the council had other ideas. She was our tsarina and could only mate the best.'

'What happened?' I was so enthralled in the story that I hardly cared that I was flying through Luska soldier after soldier.

'They mated, had my mother, then my mother mated and had me. When you are immortal, long stretches of time are not a factor. So, for the first few hundred years, the council allowed my mother's mating.'

Allowed. I didn't like the sound of that.

'Until war came knocking. A rival nation led by a male ruler set his sights on my grandmother. Offered peace for her... hand in marriage, as you would say.'

Ahh, now I could see how this story reminded her of what I was currently going through.

She was silent a while, reflecting, no doubt. I didn't want to push her, but I was desperate for the ending of this story.

'And...?' I added after a few minutes.

'Things got bad. This male did dark things to force the council's hand. They killed my grandmother's mate in order to try to force her to mate bond with this new male.'

I gasped. *'Is that possible? You said you mated for life.'*

'We do mate for life, not cemented by a ring or wedding vows but by a spiritual bonding, a sealing of two souls that is hard to describe.'

I stroked her neck. *'That's okay. I understand. So what happened to your grandmother? Did she marry the rival male?'*

I felt a profound sadness fill Liana. *'She did not. She was set to step down, make me tsarina, but the second she found out the council killed her mate for political gain, she...'*

Liana stopped talking, and I was enraptured with anticipation for the ending of the story.

Stars, don't let her stop here!

'She exploded, lashing out with every ounce of her power, which is the greatest my people have ever known. The reaction caused a tear in the fabric of space and created what you call the fire sky.'

What!

As if I couldn't be any more shocked than I was. *'What do you call it?'*

'The sky portal,' she said quietly.

My eyes nearly fell out of my head. *'Liana, what are you saying?'*

'I'm saying, young one, that the sky portal leads to my world.'

That revelation nearly made me fall off of her back.

'We were told it was an asteroid or alien rock that brought you here,' I told her.

'Close. Part of our world did break off, which is why we, older creatures who are ancient enough to remember, go along with that story. But it was my grandmother and her rage for the fallen love who was taken from her early.'

This revelation was blowing my mind, and the fact that Liana was probably the only Talanagi old enough to remember this was furthering my point.

'All Talanagi? Are they from your world?'

She nodded. *'But my specific island is only firebirds.'*

Wow. So when her grandmother exploded with magical rage, she'd pulled other creatures from outside her island and plummeted them here?

'So if you flew through the fire sky...?' I asked her.

'I tried a million times before I bonded you. I'd run out of air, die, rebirth. I've been trying to get back to my daughters since I fell.'

A sob formed in my throat at that admission. *'Liana, you have daughters still alive up there?'*

'I hope so.' Her voice was sad.

My mind went back to what she'd just said. *Before I bonded you.*

'And now that we bonded? You could theoretically breathe, right?' The entire reason creatures bonded us was to be able to leave the small confines of the Wilds and breathe outside. She could survive the fire aspect of the fire sky, or portal as she called it, but not the lack of air. But now she should be able to.

'Theoretically,' she confirmed.

I could see the capital city coming into view, and even though I was worried about Victory, and nervous about meeting Maxim and what that entailed, I had to follow this conversation through. *'Why don't you try?'* I asked in shock.

Even before she answered, I knew what she would say. *'I*

won't leave you in turmoil. I won't leave another daughter that needs me.'

My heart fissured at her words. *Daughter*. Liana was the mother of so many. Onyx, me, even Kohen, and my sisters. She was always worrying about us, protecting us, mothering us.

I couldn't say anything to that. I had no words. So instead, I leaned forward and hugged her neck, letting the cold tears slip down my cheeks and fly off into the sky. This entire time, she could have left me and gone home, and she didn't.

'I love you,' I told her as she began to descend into the center of town, where there were military personnel all gathered in a circle.

'And I, you, young one.'

I sat up, wiping my face and reeling in my emotions for the task ahead.

Liana's story about her grandmother had shocked me.

How her world fell apart did sound eerily similar to my current situation. I'd gotten emotional, and I was okay with allowing myself to cry now when I felt like it and to say those three special words. But right now I had to push all of that down and bring out the cold-hearted leader that my father raised. Empress Aisling Everhart was about to meet Prime Leader Maxim Vlek of Luska, and I was going to make that bastard release my sister or die trying.

CHAPTER
TWENTY-ONE

Aisling

I slid off of Liana, my hard boots hitting the cold ground, and stared at the group of men and women before me. They all wore Luskin red uniforms, but one had a particularly cold look to his eyes, a tall blond male with sharp features and dead black eyes. Chills ran down my spine when I looked into them.

Maxim.

'Go now,' I told Liana.

'Maybe they will let me stay. I could help—'

'Go help evacuate my people. You promised. Go, before they decide otherwise.'

Liana gave a growl of protest and then kicked off into the sky.

Maxim watched her go, the sides of his lips curling.

"She didn't want to stay for dinner?" he asked. His voice was cold and grating.

"I don't think she likes Luskin food," I told him.

He laughed, and so did every single other soldier there. But they only laughed after he did, and it was fake sounding, like puppets following their master.

"It was smart of you to come," he said as he walked over to me, circling me like a hawk.

I clenched my fists. "You didn't leave me much choice. Where is my sister?"

"Come and I'll show you." He outstretched his hand as if expecting me to take it.

Hah!

I ignored the offered hand but stepped forward, indicating I would follow him. He didn't look pleased, and the cold glare he gave me sent a shiver down my spine.

'Take my hand.' His voice boomed in my mind, and then, without my own doing, my hand moved into his. He clasped his cold fingers around mine, and my eyes flew wide.

"No," I said, trying to yank my hand away from him, but I had no power over my own limbs. He had the same power as me! That made sense. He, too, was bonded to a female firebird.

'Don't fight me,' he ordered in my mind, and I went still.

The people around us said nothing. I was worried about my sister and for my country, but I had to end this.

Now.

I tried to gather my power, to fight him and force him to stop in the same way he was forcing me. It was clear that his firebird, which I had yet to meet, had given him the same power to control people.

But when I attempted to pull for that specific power, I felt the reservoir empty.

I was still frozen, my hand in his as my eyes flew wide.

Maxim gave me an evil grin then and leaned into my ear.

"Oh, my bride-to-be, did you not feel it when I drained your power?"

No. No. No.

Had he? Was that how he did it? Was *that* his power?

Kohen's past words floated to me as if on the wind: *I just know that you lose it, that there is a time you need it, and it doesn't come to you.*

Maxim grinned ever wider. "You're trying to figure it out. How cute. Let me spell it out for you, darling." His Luskin accent was thick at some points and then nonexistent, as if he was pretending to be Amersean for me. It was weird. Leaning into my ear again, he breathed over my neck, and I felt bile rise up inside of me.

"My power is the ability to take anyone else's." He pulled away and then gestured around him. "Which is why I surround myself with such talented comrades." He laughed, and then ten seconds later, his lackeys laughed as well. He looked at me again. "Oh, but not just that. I can make your power go dormant in my presence as well, all while I'm using another person's magic. That way, you can't use it on me.

Right, Whitney?" He peered at a blonde female who wore a tight smile that didn't reach her eyes.

"Yes, sir," she quipped in a tight tone. Her eyes met mine for the briefest of seconds. There was a warning there, one that said, *Be careful.*

Message received.

This was going to be so much worse than I thought.

"You..." Maxim said, stroking my palm with his thumb and causing me to recoil, which he quickly controlled. "...are the final prize of my collection."

I peered at the others, all smiling and looking jubilant, and I felt sick.

Was he forcing those smiles with *my* power? Or did they just do it to please him? My heart sank into my stomach when I realized I'd never be free of him. If he had the power to control me, I'd never be let go.

Maybe when he's sleeping. Or maybe over time, I can learn to fight the power.

"Oh, I should warn you that Ricov can hear thoughts and transmit them to me." Maxim pointed to a big, burly man with a beard.

I paled, fear rushing through me. Had he been listening to my thoughts this whole time? What had I been thinking that might be damning?

What the hell! *Screw you, Ricov*, I thought, and watched the grin slide off his face and turn into a glare.

A small win. A small thing I had control over.

I felt Maxim's power over me loosen a bit, and I used the moment to yank my hand from his.

He reached out and grasped it, clamping down to the point of pain, and I flicked my gaze to his, feeling my whole body freeze as I fought for control. I couldn't move. I could scarcely breathe. Oh, how I'd love to just knee him in the balls right now. I would even settle for a throat punch. Anything to wipe that look off of his face. The look that said he'd won. How did he master my powers so quickly?

"Play nice," Maxim warned me, "and we will have a content life together."

Life. A life with him. I could think of nothing worse.

As we continued walking, I said nothing. Thought nothing. And when I did think things I didn't want him to know, I recited the Amersean pledge in my head over and over to cover the thoughts, make them less loud in an effort to mask them.

'Don't say anything in return,' I told Liana mentally. *'I am closing our bond because Maxim has a soldier who can read my thoughts.'* Then I closed the bond, sealing off my connection to her as I watched Ricov grin.

Bastard.

I repeated the Amersean pledge over and over again. I didn't want Liana to report anything back to me about the situation in Amersea or what I'd asked her to do. I didn't want Maxim to know anything. I felt like a prisoner in my body and my mind. To not even be able to have the freedom to think what thoughts you wanted was the ultimate horror.

My mind raced with thoughts of being stuck here in this situation for years, and I began to feel dizzy. We approached a sleek red car with a wolf and a female firebird standing in front of it, and I froze.

His two bonded.

Elaine was right. Liana was right. Kohen was right. Everyone was right. How did I get here? I was having an out-of-body experience. Things went so wrong so fast.

"Aisling..." Maxim held my hand and gestured to the wolf creature. She was white with glowing yellow ember marks and a deadly glare. "This is Misha."

I bowed my head deeply, against my will, and again, I wondered how he was doing it. I'd heard no words to force me, and he'd said nothing aloud. I was like a puppet now. He'd perfected my power on his first try. Maybe that was part of his power.

"And this is Nalika." He gestured to his firebird. My head was still bowed. He'd not allowed me up, so I just stayed that way, raging inside my body like a caged lion.

I would kill this bastard. I would rip his head from his body!

"*Tsk tsk*, naughty thoughts for your future husband," Maxim said.

Screw you, I thought, and instead of letting my head up, I was forced to kneel. My legs gave out as he finally let go of my hand so that I could fall onto my palms. On my hands and knees, I touched my forehead to his feet.

"So obedient," Maxim said and laughed.

The dozen or so soldiers around us laughed, too, and at that moment, I wanted to cry. I was trapped in a nightmare.

"Take me to my sister. Please," I begged.

His hold over me broke, and I was allowed to stand. When I did, he was grinning at me. "Ohh, I *do* like the word 'please'. That will go far with me. You will learn. Right, Whitney?" He looked at the blonde again, and she nodded.

"Yes, sir."

I didn't know what she'd done to incur his attention, but it clearly wasn't good. She was shooting eye daggers at the back of his head. Maxim opened the car door, and I stepped inside of my own free will as he, his wolf, Whitney, and Ricov, got in behind me. We all spread out along the seats facing each other, very similar to my family car.

The car took off, and we rode in awkward silence as I prayed my sister was unharmed.

"So long as you cooperate with our little agreement, your sister will live a long and happy life here. I have a younger boy in mind who we can betroth her to," Maxim said.

I tried not to react, repeating an old saying we used to spout as children. *Sticks and stones can break my bones, but words will never hurt me.* Anything to keep him from knowing my thoughts. The saying looped in my mind loudly over and over as I panicked about him marrying off my little sister.

Maxim's head snapped to Whitney, and the woman paled. She was in her mid-twenties, beautiful in an understated way. There was a strength in her he hadn't beaten out. Yet.

"After all I've done for you, you still think that way about me?" he asked her. I wondered what Whitney had thought, and suddenly, I felt an unspoken alliance with the woman.

"Forgive me, sir," she said sweetly, fakeness dripping from her voice.

He waved his hand at her as if annoyed, and I wondered why she was with us.

Ricov was clearly here so that Maxim could read our thoughts, but what was her gift? I wondered.

Maxim grinned at me. "Oh, you'll see."

I sighed, sad that I no longer had privacy with my own thoughts. Everything was under his control. My body, my mind, my free will.

Visions of our wedding night bloomed in my head, and I went numb, sinking into a deep sadness that I wasn't sure I could ever crawl out of.

We drove through the downtown area, passing large buildings, and then finally past where the Red Palace used to be. It was cleared land now, already halfway through rebuilding, this time from steel.

I glanced at Maxim to see him watching me.

"That night, you made all my dreams come true," he said wistfully.

The night I killed his father was the night all his dreams came true? That was telling of his character, or lack thereof.

I glanced at Ricov, ready to have him send that thought to Maxim, but Maxim seemed preoccupied with Whitney. He stared at her and she glared back at him, and tension filled the car, the kind that did when you were former or current lovers.

Interesting.

I stared back out the window, taking in all the sights and

wondering how far we would have to travel to see my sister, what conditions she was being kept in, and how the hell I was going to survive this new life.

I suddenly had a thought. Maxim had taken my power to control, but he hadn't taken my power to explode. If I detonated myself right now, I could kill us all and—

Maxim's hand snaked out and wrapped around my throat, pinching off my air supply. I tried to reach up and pry it off, but he forced my hands to remain down.

"If you try to end my life in any way, the men I have holding your sister will kill her as I have instructed them to. Do you understand me?"

I nodded, able to move my head, and then he let go, leaving me gasping and sputtering for air.

My gaze flicked to Whitney, who appeared horrified at my treatment. But when Maxim peered at her, the look was gone, and she appeared unfazed.

Ricov stared out the window at the passing trees as if nothing had happened.

Sticks and stones may break my bones, but words will never hurt me, I repeated over and over as I tried to process what had just happened.

I'd learned something. I *was* able to kill Maxim. That plan would indeed work, or he wouldn't have freaked out.

Sticks and stones may break my bones, but words will never hurt me.

Ricov glared at me with a confused look on his face, as if he couldn't read my thoughts clearly when I chanted the nursery rhyme.

I grinned. *Checkmate, you bastard.*

The car pulled off the main road and onto one that led to a huge set of iron gates. The forest was thick here, and it looked like a manor had been carved out of it. I peered up at the sky to see Maxim's firebird flying over us and to a house that sat atop the hill.

I peered at the wolf, who was also staring at me.

I'd never felt so helpless in all my life.

Two guards at the gate both had griffin Talanagi. They waved us in, opening the gates. By my count, we'd driven about thirty minutes north of the Red Palace.

As we wound up the road, I took in the palatial home. In any other circumstance, I'd say it was beautiful, but I was pretty sure it was about to become my prison.

"The wedding will be here tomorrow." Maxim pointed to a well-manicured garden where some white silk tents were being erected.

My stomach roiled.

Sticks and stones may break my bones, but words will never hurt me.

"It's beautiful," I said, coming from the angle of a complacent prisoner.

Sticks and stones may break my bones, but words will never hurt me.

He nodded, as if pleased with my response. "I'm glad you think so. The treaty for the peaceful surrender of your people and lands is being drawn up by my council and will be ready before the wedding."

Sticks and stones may break my bones, but words will never hurt me.

Sticks and stones may break my bones, but words will never hurt me.

Emotion clogged my throat, and tears filled my eyes.

Kohen. I couldn't help but think of him in this moment.

I'll always protect you.

This time, he was wrong. No one could protect me from this. The best I could hope for was saving my people and my sisters.

Sticks and stones may break my bones, but words will never hurt me.

My gaze flicked to Ricov, and he rolled his eyes. It was getting hard to chant and think at the same time.

The car pulled up to the mansion. Maxim stepped out, and we all followed. I quickly did a scan to see that there were over a dozen guards patrolling the area. The two at the door both had lion creatures.

They bowed deeply as Maxim approached, and I wondered if they did it of their own free will. Ricov opened the large double doors and then Maxim stepped inside, gesturing widely to the grand home.

"Welcome home, Aisling," he said, and I tried not to show my disgust.

The foyer we stood in had dark slate floors and red wallpaper that led all the way up to a double staircase, which held a second level. It was not my taste, but you couldn't deny the grandness.

"This was all my father's design, but if you want to redecorate, I can arrange for that," Maxim said.

I glared at Ricov, who had clearly shared my thoughts on the design.

"I'm an empress, a warrior," I growled. "I'm not a decorator."

Maxim's lip curled as if he liked my feistiness a little bit. "Which is why I chose you. Our children will be very powerful."

Sticks and stones may break my bones, but words will never hurt me.

Sticks and stones may break my bones, but words will never hurt me.

I tried desperately to cover up my feelings for that statement. I'd rather me and all my sisters die than bear this demon a child. Maxim's eyes thinned to slits, and I knew he'd heard that thought.

"Let's go see your sister, shall we? Maybe that will motivate you to behave."

I felt sick to my stomach as anger and rage washed over me. If she was hurt, I wasn't sure I would be able to control my reaction. I might explode and kill us all.

Maxim reached out and took my hand, freezing it in his palm as he led me down the hallway. My heart thumped wildly with each step. The fight to kidnap Victory had been bloody. Elaine almost died and could be dead for all I knew. If they hurt Victory...

Smoke began to rise off of my skin. Maxim turned his head ever so slowly to look at me. "Stop it," he commanded in an even but firm tone. The smoke dissipated, and I felt my powers freeze.

Dammit. He'd figured out how to use my one power to control the other.

He shot me a smug grin, but it never reached his eyes. They were like two cold, dark pits. If I stared at them too long, I got chills.

There was a male guard standing in front of a bedroom door, with a wolf creature beside him. He bowed to Maxim and then opened the door. I steeled myself, prepared for my sister to be bloody and chained to a chair with a gag over her mouth. But when the door opened and we stepped inside, I was shocked.

Victory looked up from where she'd been sitting on a pale pink rug and talking to another girl her age. She looked freshly washed, in a clean blue dress, and unharmed.

"Aisling!" she sobbed and ran to me.

Maxim allowed me to walk to her and open my arms. We crashed together as I had a vague knowledge of the other little girl running to Whitney for a hug.

Was that her sister?

"Maxim can hear your thoughts when Ricov is around," I whispered into her ear and flicked my gaze to the bearded bastard at the door.

She pulled back, fearfully looking at both Maxim and then Ricov.

"Is Elaine...? Are Valor and Virtue... alive?"

I nodded. "All of them."

It wasn't a lie. Elaine *was* alive when I left.

She sagged in relief, almost sinking to the floor.

"Are you hurt? Hungry? Have they been treating you okay?" I asked her.

She nodded. "I'm fine. They feed us and let us bathe. They said I will start lessons tomorrow and live here from now on." Her voice caught, her face begging me to answer that question: *Is this our life now?*

Maxim smiled at my sister. "That's right, Victory. Your sister is going to surrender in the war, and we are going to get married, unite our people, and bring peace."

Her eyes widened in fear. She looked at me, and Maxim forced my head to nod.

"No." Victory moaned, clutching her chest. "Our home, my sisters."

"Your sisters are welcome to join you here," Maxim said coyly.

"No," I growled.

Maxim shrugged. "Suit yourself."

I stroked Victory's hair. "Everything is going to be okay," I told her.

She opened her mouth to speak, probably with a hundred questions on her tongue, but then looked from Ricov to Maxim and closed it.

"Okay," she said, dejected.

"Who is this?" I asked Victory, pointing to the thirteen- or fourteen-year-old girl with blonde hair who was standing next to Whitney. Now that I looked at them closely, I could see they were sisters.

"This is my new friend, Ana," Victory said hesitantly.

Ana waved to me, and I shared a tense smile with Whitney. So much was unsaid between us. We both wanted to keep our sisters safe. And we both hated Maxim.

"Well, I'm glad you're not alone here," I told Victory in a pleasant voice, trying to go along with things and not anger Maxim.

Ana and Victory both nodded.

"Alright, we've got one more stop before dinner," Maxim announced, and then all of a sudden, I was backing out of the room against my will.

"Don't leave!" Victory ran for me, crying. Maxim threw his hand out, and Victory froze mid-step, eyes wide.

"Don't hurt her!" I screamed. My voice was my own, but my movements were not. I was still backing out of the room, and I'd just reached the doorway. Ricov and Whitney, followed by Maxim, were next. Both Victory and Ana were frozen in place, tears streaming down their faces.

"No one's hurt. We're just laying down some authority." Maxim smiled at me. "Have a good night, girls. Be good so your sisters won't have an *accident*," he told them and then shut the door.

"You didn't have to scare them like that," I spat.

The girls pounded against the door, and my gaze flicked to Whitney. What I saw there gave me hope. There was a cold, calculating look in her eye. A quiet, simmering fury. She was planning something. I peered down to see her pinching the outside of her thigh. It was barely noticeable, but I saw her do it when the slight movement drew my gaze. Why would she be pinching herself unless... Did pain keep Ricov from hearing our thoughts?

"Shall we go to the testing site now, Prime Leader?" Ricov asked Maxim.

Maxim nodded.

Ricov seemed too preoccupied with Maxim to have read my thoughts.

We all walked down the hallway then in unison, Whitney and my feet matching cadence with Maxim. He was clearly controlling us both, and I hated every second of it, but I was at a loss for what to do. I couldn't even think properly with Ricov around.

I just let go and let Maxim control me. Anything to keep Victory safe.

I hated who I'd become, from strong leader to loyal puppet.

CHAPTER TWENTY-TWO

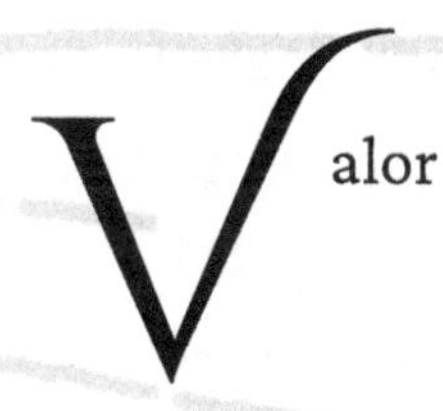

Valor

Sorak was a nice city, but I couldn't enjoy the sights while Elaine lay dying back home, and my sister was a prisoner of war. I paced the carpet in the large home that Tej and Arjun had brought Virtue and me to. Anika and Meera were here, my sister's friends from boot camp. But I was too overwhelmed to really talk to anyone. I just wanted my family back together. One second, we'd been driving to Sky Reach, and then the next, a dragon landed on our car, tossing us off the road. I thought now that I had a creature, I'd be a badass fighter and be able to protect my sisters, but it turned out I was a healer who couldn't heal under stress. My throat pinched as I thought of Elaine bleeding out in the woods while I was helpless to stop it.

'You did the best you could. You are still learning,' Zara told me from the backyard, where she patrolled with the other creatures.

'I failed everyone,' I corrected her.

"Hey," Arjun entered the room with Anika. He was holding a plate of food. "You should eat something."

"Thanks, but I'm not hungry," I told him, continuing my pacing. Maybe I should take Zara back to Amersea and help Aisling. I felt better now, less rattled. Maybe my healing gift would return.

"Valor, right?" Anika approached me with a kind smile. "I don't think I've officially met you, but I've heard about you from Aisling."

The moment I looked at her, I knew there was something broken about her. It was like with Tetra—I couldn't focus on her face when her foot was calling to me. I hated to call someone *broken*; it felt rude, but that's what I saw. I saw people now as puzzles with pieces missing. Tetra's missing piece was in her foot, and Anika was missing a piece in her head.

"Something's wrong with your brain," I blurted out.

Anika's eyes flew wide, and I winced. "I'm sorry, I just meant..."

Crap. Subtlety was not something I had mastered yet.

"Did your sister tell you?" Anika asked me.

I frowned, unable to look away from her brain. It was like a picture in my mind getting clearer and clearer every second. Little noodles that were supposed to be connected were not in her case.

"Tell me what?" I asked dreamily, taking a step closer to her and cocking my head. I could see the noodle-like strands of energy that were broken, and where they were broken, there was no light. It was a dead zone.

I sounded crazy. I knew that. But that was what I saw.

Anika was watching me, and I pulled my gaze away from her head and met her eyes. "I'm so sorry. I have a new gift that I'm still learning how to—"

"She's a healer," Virtue said from the doorway.

Anika's mouth popped open, and she reached up and touched the hair at her temple. "Oh. Well, I've been to healers before. What I have I was born with and can't be healed."

I'd heard that before.

My hands began to heat up, and then I felt Zara at the window behind me.

'No, I don't want to do this right now,' I told her. Golden arcs of light began to shoot off my palms, and Arjun gasped.

"Tej!" He called for his older brother.

'I don't think we control this gift,' Zara told me, and that broke my heart. So I couldn't save Elaine, who was like a mother to me, but my power wanted to save some stranger from Imbria?

It wasn't fair.

Anika's brain, her puzzle, her missing piece, the broken noodles, they surged unbidden in my mind.

"She fully healed Tetra's foot," my sister said, and the entire energy of the room changed.

The Imbrian girl walked towards me suddenly and then fell to her knees in front of me, eyes filling with tears. "Please," she whimpered, and my heart shattered.

I might not be able to control the gift, but I wouldn't deny it to anyone either. That was not within me.

I nodded, placing my glowing hands on her head. The energy that I saw as broken noodles flared to life when I touched her, and a splitting headache overcame me. I hadn't felt anything before, standing near her like I had with Tetra, but now that I was touching her, it hurt.

I hissed, pulling the broken energy noodles together and mending them with the golden light.

"What the stars?" Tej said, but I ignored him.

The door opened, and I felt Zara at my back. She was like a piece of ember, charging me up when my golden magic ran low. We were both still learning how this worked.

I pieced the energy in Anika's head together, threading noodles in to fill the black gaps, and my headache eased. When I was all done, the golden energy fell away from me, and I popped my eyes open.

We all just sat there, silent and unsure of what to say. This wasn't like Tetra's healing, where we could see the results.

"I felt that," Anika said dreamily, standing. "Did you... am I healed?"

I looked at her. All the puzzle pieces were in order now. I nodded.

"Thank you." She pulled me into a hug, and I patted her back awkwardly. I wasn't used to this.

"I should fly back and see if I can help my sister," I told everyone.

Zara nudged my leg. *'Stay here. Kohen and Onyx are coming with Elaine.'*

My head snapped to her. "What?" I asked my creature aloud.

'Go outside,' she told me.

I rushed out front of the house and into the street filled with mansions just like it. Peering up, I noticed Onyx, Kohen's dragon, but she wasn't alone. There were three people riding her. Kohen was one, the healer he had brought was the other, and—

"Elaine!" Virtue yelled, running out into the cobblestone street.

Onyx landed, and Elaine, who was pale and weary-looking, slid off of him and pulled out a cane made of a broken tree branch.

Virtue and I both ran to her, embracing her lightly so as not to cause any more wounds.

"I'm sorry," Elaine told us, her voice rough. "I'm sorry I allowed them to take Victory."

I shook my head. "You fought as best you could. We all did. Are you okay?"

She let out a shuddering breath. "I need... to rest. But I will be."

"I'll take you inside." Meera, the small and unassuming Imbrian girl, walked up and hooked arms with Elaine.

Where was Aisling?

Elaine reached out, caressing the side of my face and then Virtue's, and nodded. "I'm so sorry."

She'd lost Vespa. Victory. Our driver, Verik. I couldn't imagine how she felt.

"It's okay," I told her.

"Valor Everhart." Kohen's voice was formal behind me.

I turned, wondering why he was acting like that. He was wearing a cold mask of steel as he handed me a letter.

"Your sister went after Victory. I gave her my solemn vow that I would not let you be harmed. Read this letter, then we need to evacuate your people. I will stay with you the entire time to make sure you are safe."

My eyebrows nearly hit my hairline.

What did he just say?

Evacuate my people? *Why?*

Kohen walked away then, and Tej ran after him.

"What do we do?" he asked his brother.

Kohen straddled Onyx. "Prepare for hundreds of thousands of refugees. Tell the adjoining cities and villages. And *don't* cross that border into Amersea. Promise me."

"But—"

"Promise me!" Kohen snapped.

Tej promised, and I looked down at the letter. I was too much in shock to argue or say anything.

When I opened it and read it, my heart fell into my stomach.

. . .

Valor,

There is nothing I wouldn't do to keep you girls safe. So please forgive me now for having to marry Maxim to keep Virtue safe.

I stopped reading for a moment. Marry Maxim!

You will be interim empress while I'm gone. I'm sorry you are having to take this on so young, but Luska has threatened to bomb Riverine. You need to order a mass evacuation. Trust Kohen and the Imbrians. Father lied about the Great Blackout. It wasn't Imbria. It was him. Stay strong and take care of Virtue. I love you.

Aisling

.

It wasn't Imbria. It was him.

It was him.

I staggered backward, handing Virtue the letter.

Father was the one who killed thousands of our people? *No.* He was mean, but he wasn't evil. Right?

Virtue read the letter next to me, tears streaming down her cheeks and onto the paper. All these years, we'd blamed an innocent man for something he never did. Not just him—we'd blamed all of Imbria. I felt sick, but I had no time to process the fact that my father was a monster.

I'd just become empress at fourteen years old.

Stars help me.

Zara dropped to one knee beside me, and I mounted her, preparing to move my people from the home they'd always loved and known into a place they had always seen as enemy territory. Luksa had threatened Riverine? Then we had to evacuate our people, like Aisling said.

How was I going to do this without Aisling? Without Elaine? I wasn't trained for this.

"I'll be by your side every step of the way," Kohen said. "I have a letter from your sister to the admirals in her Fleet. I'd like you to help me deliver it so that maybe they won't shoot me down before I can hand it to them." He smiled at the joke, and I chuckled, feeling a bit more lighthearted. I could see now how Aisling had seen something in him. If I put all the prejudices I had away, and rumors I'd heard of the Badshah family, Kohen had been so helpful it was hard to hang onto any lies I was raised with about him.

I had to trust what I could see from now on, not what I'd been told.

"Okay. Let's go," I said, and Virtue ran over to me, hugging my leg. "Be careful." Her voice broke. "You're all I have left."

That statement hit me like a steam train. Victory was gone. Aisling was gone. Virtue and I were all that remained of the Everhart line.

With that, Zara ascended into the sky, and I took up my responsibilities, missing the days when my biggest worry was how my hair looked.

CHAPTER TWENTY-THREE

A isling

Whitney kept doing that thing where she would pinch the outside of her thigh every so often. I was now convinced it was for a purpose, and I'd started doing it, too, practicing with certain thoughts as I did it.

I hate you, Ricov, you bastard. I hope you eat cow dung for the rest of your life, I thought as I inflicted pain on myself.

Ricov stared uncaring out the window, and I peered at Whitney. Her gaze flicked down to my thigh, where I had just been pinching, and she nodded once.

Aha!

So this was the way to keep him out. I felt immense relief

at knowing there was a way to keep my thoughts to myself when I wanted to. I wasn't breaking the skin, just enough to give my system a jolt of pain. A small price to pay to be able to strategize and think on my own. I'd have to let normal thoughts through every so often, so Ricov wasn't suspicious, but I was feeling marginally better about my situation.

The drive took over an hour before we reached a remote stretch of land, where we pulled off the main roadway and into some sort of military installation. Throughout the drive, I'd allowed normal curious thoughts of the scenery to come through loud and clear and then inflicted small amounts of pain on myself to have private thoughts. Thoughts of escape, of getting word to Kohen, of my sisters.

I felt a bond with Whitney through our shared experience, though we hadn't even had a conversation. Our sisters were both captive. We were in this together, even if we were on opposing sides of the war.

There were soldiers and creatures all over the military base as we pulled up to a gate. The trees had been hacked down so that it was just a wide-open field in the middle of the forest. No homes or towns stood nearby, and there was only a single large industrial building.

The guard at the gate saluted Maxim as we passed, and I watched as each soldier on base turned to face the red car, saluting as we drove by.

Their boss was here.

I found myself wondering if Elaine had pulled through surgery. If Virtue and Valor had made it to Imbria okay. If my people were being evacuated in the off chance this whole thing with Maxim ended badly. Which I was a hundred percent sure was going to happen. All these thoughts I kept to myself by digging my fingers into my palm.

"Why are we here?" I asked Maxim in a calm, curious tone.

Maxim peered at Whitney with a grin. "Sergeant Whitney has a big role to fulfill. Don't you?"

She paled, fear flashing in her eyes. "Sir, with all due respect to your authority and final say, I still think having a weapon of this level of destruction is contrary to the ongoing survival of humanity."

My stomach dropped at her statement. The survival of humanity was threatened by a weapon they had? *Stars*, was that the one from his letter?

"Your disagreement has been noted. But so long as *we* wield this weapon, Luska will survive just fine. I'm not worried about anyone else, and if you want your sister to remain safe, you will activate it for testing."

Whitney nodded curtly, but I noticed the way her nails dug into her palm. I allowed my trepidation of this new weapon to leak into my thoughts so that Ricov wouldn't know I was hiding them.

What was it? Was it the same bomb that Maxim had written about in his letter to me? The one that could flatten Amersea?

Had he bluffed when the weapon wasn't even fully ready yet? It sounded like it. And I'd played right into his hand. Not that I'd had a choice. He had Victory.

When the car parked, we stepped out. Maxim immediately grasped my hand as soldiers craned their necks to look at us.

I wondered what they thought of me. About to surrender my lands and my people. Did I look weak? Did they know it was to save my sister?

We stepped inside the large warehouse building. A large circular metal object sat in the middle of the room, looming ten feet high. It looked like a huge cannonball. There were rivets at the seams, but even so, I could see something glowing inside.

Ember.

"Ember isn't combustible," I said in confusion. We'd tried to make ember bombs, but when struck, it just broke apart into smaller pieces. It was like coal but burned much longer and naturally.

Maxim grinned, finally letting my hand go. "That's where our lovely Whitney comes into play. Her gift is that she can mutate the properties of something, and we recently learned she can make the smallest piece of ember explode like a firework. Isn't that right, Sergeant?"

Guilt and shame washed over Whitney's face. "Yes, sir."

"And now we get to see what happens with a big piece." Maxim rubbed his hands together and began to walk over to his men. I had planned on staying back, but my legs began to move, unbidden by me, and I followed him.

Controlling bastard.

"Everything all set for the test?" Maxim asked one of his men, who was screwing some lid on the top of the metal ball.

"Yes, sir," the man said, his gaze flicking to me. He glared at me, not even bothering to hide his hatred.

Maxim seemed to pick up on it. Leaning into me, he whispered against my neck. "When you blew up the Red Palace, you killed Sergei's father, too."

Crap. My stomach dropped. I was probably not going to survive long here. If Maxim didn't kill me, someone would.

Maxim looked surprised, and I realized I hadn't hidden that thought, and Ricov was lurking in his usual lurker ways.

"Oh, my little pet. I won't let anything happen to you. Ever. You are my greatest trophy."

Maxim leaned in to kiss my cheek. I tried to move away, but he held me there. His cold, slightly damp lips pressed to my cheek, and I inwardly cringed.

Clenching my fists, I dug my nails into my palms. I missed Kohen. I missed *his* kisses, I missed making love to him for the first time, and I missed being *his* wife. This new reality was devastating. I wasn't sure how much longer I could take it.

You are my greatest trophy. Normal people collected painted rocks. Maxim collected people. Liana was right when she said he didn't have a soul. This demon was dead inside. I was sure of it. And as long as I was alive, he had my power. I couldn't even die because he had my sister.

It all felt so hopeless.

We walked outside, my steps in perfect synch with Whitney's as Maxim's soldiers rolled the giant spherical bomb out behind us.

I watched as Whitney walked over to the bomb with

puppet-like steps and laid her hands on it. A single tear slid down her face as she bowed her head and rested it on the bomb. I hadn't noticed it before, but an eagle creature screeched above us. Was it hers? It seemed agitated, as if warning her not to do this. Her hands glowed a sickly green, and I wondered if it was really her doing this, or Maxim, or a little of both. I wasn't judging. I'd do the same for Victory or any one of my sisters.

The metal glowed that same sickly green, and then Whitney staggered backward, breathless. The eagle above us cried out, and now I was sure it was her creature. Heat washed over me like an invisible fire, and I stepped forward, Maxim clearly allowing it. I was shocked to find the source of the heat was the ember ball. She'd... definitely activated it in some way.

"Professor," Maxim said, and an older man wearing civilian clothes stepped over to the ball, holding his hands out.

I cocked my head to the side, curious as to what was going to happen, and then Maxim forced my legs to step backward. I hated the feeling of my body moving without my permission.

"You can ask me to move," I growled at him.

"Where's the fun in that?" he sneered.

That sick feeling was back in my stomach. I dreaded being alone with him and began to panic. Then the ball started levitating, and all thoughts flew out of my head.

The professor had his hands up and seemed to be guiding the giant bomb up and out into the open field.

"Sir, we should go back inside. There could be debris," a soldier told Maxim. He nodded, and then Whitney and I were walking in tandem, against our will, at Maxim's side. Now I saw why she was so important to him. His dangerous weapon was nothing without her. And he couldn't control anyone without me.

I realized I was digging my fingers into my palms so hard that I'd drawn blood. Relaxing, I wiped them on my pants and took a cleansing breath. Once we were back inside the building, they pulled down a rolling steel door with a small viewing slit inside of it.

The professor was still concentrating on moving the sphere, but he was also backing up closer to the building we were in. I watched as he slipped inside through an open side door. Sweat beaded his brow, as if doing this was taking tremendous force out of him. I could imagine it was.

When the bomb was a speck on the horizon, hovering over some thick, uninhabited forest, Maxim nodded. "Drop it."

The man hesitated for a second, as if weighing the consequences of those actions. We all peered through the slit in the metal door in anticipation.

"Drop it!" Maxim shouted so loudly I startled. The ball plummeted and was lost in the trees. I braced myself. But nothing could have prepared me for what happened next.

CHAPTER
TWENTY-FOUR

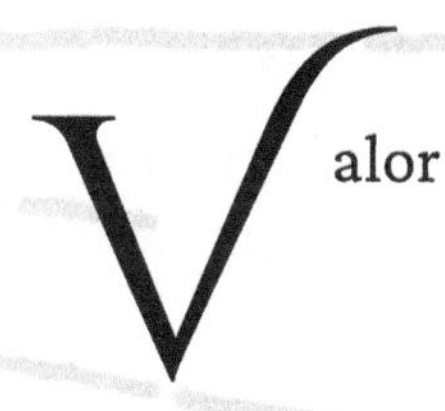

Valor

I THOUGHT I'd lost my innocence in the Wilds, but I was wrong. It was standing before my sister's council of admirals as the interim empress that my childhood died. I'd never again be that slightly carefree girl who snuck out and stole cookies from the kitchen or thought of ways to prank Elaine. Young Valor was dead. Now, I had to become Aisling. Perfect strong Aisling. I'd never be as good as her, but I could try.

Commander Ledger read the note Kohen gave him with wide eyes, and then he peered over at me.

"I need to swear you in. Temporarily," he said.

I nodded.

"She's a child!" Admiral Caruso argued.

"Does she even have a power? She didn't start boot camp yet. She's untrained," Admiral Blade growled.

My sister once told me that being empress was fifty percent confidence, fifty percent fake it until you make it. I was going to have to do that now.

"Are you questioning my eldest sister's authority? Her judgment?" I asked Admiral Blade.

He shrugged. "Are you really going to lead us into battle, sweetheart? Are you even out of a training bra?"

Oh hell no.

Moving quickly, I pulled a small throwing knife from my waist and launched it at the admiral, skimming his ear.

The room erupted into shouts and gasps of surprise. Admiral Blade touched the blood droplet at his ear and peered at me with shock.

"You bi—"

"I'd watch your tongue if I were you," Kohen told him. "I'd like to take this time to remind the council that Empress Valor rides a Talanagi. Something *none* of you do."

That made silence fall over the room.

As stressful as this was, I had to admit that Empress Valor had a nice ring to it.

"Why are you even here, Badshah?" Ledger asked Kohen.

"That's *King* Badshah to you, Commander," I reminded Commander Ledger, and his jaw ticced a little.

Kohen looked like he was trying to suppress a smile. "Because my wife asked me—"

"Your what!?" I screamed, peering over at Kohen in shock.

The admirals in the room didn't seem fazed by his comment, but I'd been blown back by it. Was he talking about my sister?

Kohen turned to me. "Aisling and I married in secret a few days ago." Then he faced the admirals. "And I would do *anything* to protect her lands and people. Come to Imbria until we can figure out a plan to subdue Maxim and his bomb." Kohen gestured to the letter, which I was guessing explained everything he was talking about.

"You would do anything?" Admiral Blade asked Kohen.

"Anything," Kohen agreed.

The commander and Admiral Blade shared a look, and then the commander peered at Kohen. "Would you join Amersea again? One nation?"

"Yes. I believe that we are stronger together. We must join against Luska. I would be happy to unite our countries together again, but it won't be like it was last time. Imbria won't be fed scraps from the Fleet. We will build more bases in Imbria to beef up forces there. We will take Amersean tax money and rebuild all that you have bombed and broken and taken from us. Imbrians will be able to freely move to Amersea if they please, and vice versa. We will be seen as one, with Aisling and I ruling over it all together."

The men bristled a little at that, but I thought it sounded beautiful and more than fair.

"That seems fair." Admiral Caruso offered. "And if Luska

has a bomb they plan to drop on Riverine, we should evacuate temporarily."

The commander was skeptical of Kohen: "If I draft up everything you just said in writing, you would sign it today?"

Kohen nodded. "But I would ask that we wait to enact any measures until Aisling can go over the agreement as well to make sure she is happy with it."

I inwardly swooned at how protective and caring he was being for my sister, even though she wasn't here.

"Aisling may never come back again," Admiral Blade said.

"She's coming back," Kohen growled. "I just haven't figured out how yet."

The room was silent for a moment, everyone lost in their thoughts.

"I will sign the agreement in Aisling's place, with a clause that if—*when*—she returns and doesn't like anything we have agreed upon, she can modify it," I said. "Let's get this bureaucracy over with and start the evacuation. I'd hate for innocent civilians to die while we are signing papers." That got everyone moving.

People got up from the table and began moving to the edges of the room, taking out papers and huddling in the corners, whispering.

Kohen pulled me aside and gave me a small smile. "You did well. Aisling would be proud."

I gave a nervous laugh. "Thanks. I felt like I was going to be sick talking to Admiral Blade like that."

Kohen chuckled, but then his smile faltered.

I frowned, lowering my voice. "Have you seen Aisling come home? You know... with your gift?" I knew from his letter and what his brothers said in the Wilds that he could see the future. I was desperately hoping he'd seen Aisling come home.

He sighed, looking tortured. "Not yet. But... there are many paths that branch out in all different directions. I just need to find one that brings her home to me alive."

My gut clenched at the word *alive*. Had he seen her brought home dead? I didn't have the courage to ask.

"You see many outcomes?" I hadn't thought that was possible, but now it made sense. We all made decisions every day, and each one might lead to a different world.

Kohen nodded. "But none of them show your sister..." He trailed off, and it felt like my heart stopped.

"What about sneaking in there? Just you, go through the Wilds like we did—"

"I get killed. She stays Maxim's prisoner. They have too many soldiers constantly watching for that. In the sky and on the ground."

Dammit. No.

My mind raced. I wasn't as good at strategy as Aisling, but I had played the same strategy games with Elaine. I just needed to think of something that—

I perked up. "What if I created a distraction?"

Kohen seemed to consider it. "It would have to be a huge distraction, Valor, and I can't condone you doing anything. Aisling would never forgive me if anything happened to you."

"I'm not a child!" I snapped. "Not anymore. And it wouldn't just be me. It would be the Fleet, which I'm in charge of until Aisling gets home."

Kohen chewed the inside of his lip. "I don't know. I haven't seen that outcome."

I rolled my eyes. "Maybe you have to trust, Kohen. You can't wait for a vision to move in life. My sister could be dead by then. Just hear me out."

He paled at that statement. "Okay. What do you have in mind?"

Aisling was going to kill me when she got home, but if she got home to yell at me, it was worth it.

"We draw their forces west," I told him.

"West?" Kohen balked. "How are you going to get there? By boat? They'll sink you before you can even pass the Wall. Amersea has never attacked from the west for that reason."

I nodded. "But now we have over two dozen flying Talanagi. We draw them west while you sneak in from the east and save Aisling and Victory."

Kohen's mouth popped open. "No offense, Valor, but you and a bunch of untrained, barely bonded, not-even-sworn-into-the-Fleet-yet *kids* are going to lure the entire Luskin army west? It's suicide."

'We could drop a bomb like you and Aisling did on the Red Palace in Luska,' Zara said. *'But on their west army base. It will draw all the attention.'*

I relayed Zara's idea to Kohen, and he reached up and rubbed his temples.

"It's too dangerous."

Another idea popped into my head. “What if I flew with Tetra? She could create a shield around our small group and protect us...”

I could see that he was warming to the idea.

“Kohen, are you really going to let Aisling marry that psycho?” I asked him.

He looked anguished. “Stars, I hope not. Okay. We’ll do it. But we have to convince the admirals. And we have to evacuate Amersea first because there will be retaliation.”

I peered at the admirals and nodded. “Leave them to me.” I might not be as powerful as Aisling, but I’d spent years learning the art of getting my way, and I planned to do that now. My eldest sister sacrificed a lot for us. I wasn’t about to let her marry the prime leader of Luska against her will.

CHAPTER TWENTY-FIVE

Aisling

When the steel ball dropped into the trees, based on what Kohen said, I'd expected an explosion in the distance and a crater, but I hadn't been prepared for the carnage that followed.

The force of the blast instantly blew the steel doors open, and everyone standing in front of them was knocked backward. Including me.

My elbow hit the ground first, a sharp pain shooting up my arm, and I cried out. Maxim half fell on top of me, worsening the force put on my arm. My ears rang as the blast reached us; the force of its power was like I'd been slapped in the face.

That far off? How? Nothing I'd seen in my life was that powerful. Not even the explosive we dropped on the Red Palace. I peered around the room in a daze, and my gaze landed on Whitney. She was staring out at the massive crater that had formed in the woods, the size of a city. Broken trees formed concentric circles around it all the way to the building we were in. A huge mushroom cloud of dust rose up from where the weapon had been dropped.

Tears fell down her face. Her words came back to haunt me now.

Having a weapon of this level of destruction is contrary to the ongoing survival of humanity.

Whitney was right. One of these bombs could wipe out hundreds of thousands in a highly populated city. Of *my* city. *Riverine*. My gaze then flicked to Maxim, who was staring out at the carnage with pure joy, and my stomach dropped. He looked like a proud father watching his child take their first few steps.

Bile rose in my throat; my elbow pinged with fresh pain. Some of the soldiers began clapping and whooping, and Maxim stood. He faced each one, chin high and proud as I struggled to sit up. Something was wrong with my elbow, and my ears were still ringing.

Maxim finally realized I hadn't gotten up and peered down at me. "Are you injured, little pet?" he called down to me in a demeaning tone.

I glared up at him, holding my probably broken elbow to

my chest. "I'm fine," I growled, standing and swaying on my feet a little.

"She's in pain," Ricov said, and I glared at the giant oaf.

"Medic!" Maxim snapped his fingers, and someone ran to my side. Then Maxim and Ricov went over to speak to the professor who'd levitated the ball.

A female medic came over to me and set a bag down. "Can you straighten your arm?"

There was still chaos everywhere, people getting up and trying to lift fallen furniture. Ricov stood beside Maxim and the professor and Whitney... I noticed Whitney was scribbling feverishly on a piece of paper and glancing at Ricov and Maxim. With one hand, she wrote, and with the other, she dug into a cut that had opened on her arm.

What was she writing? I tried to extend my elbow, and a fresh wave of pain came over me, causing me to cry out.

Maxim peered back at me, and I gave him a little wave of apology, letting him know I was okay and hopefully keeping his attention away from Whitney.

Maxim went back to speaking to Ricov, and then Whitney stood, limping as she made her way over to me.

"Can you look at my ankle after you are done with her?" Whitney asked the medic, slipping something into my pocket.

I stayed eerily still, wanting so badly to read the note, but it wasn't safe right now.

"Bone healer!" the female medic cried out loudly. A man who had a cut above his eyebrow ran over to me, and the female medic moved on to Whitney.

"Your elbow is broken." The man's accent was so thick I barely understood him.

I nodded. "Cast it. I'll be fine."

He shook his head. "I'll fix." He snapped his fingers, and a large red dragon appeared outside the blasted-open doors.

I wasn't used to seeing so many Talanagi. They had them everywhere, and I was just now realizing it meant the Luskin people had way more powerful gifts than we did.

He was clearly a "bone healer," which was so incredibly rare in Amersea. But people here didn't seem fazed by it.

He guided me outside, and when I got within ten feet of Maxim, he broke away from the people he'd been talking to and came to stand at my side. "Don't want you getting lost, little pet," he told me with a grin.

I wondered if there was a physical proximity element to his magic, but my thoughts didn't linger there too long.

I watched as the bone healer and his accompanying dragon creature healed my wound and noted it was very similar to Valor's magic.

When he was done, he left, and then Maxim was there staring at the giant hole in the earth, far more destruction than anything I'd ever seen.

He turned to face me with absolute glee on his face. "With this, I can conquer not only Amersea but Imbria too."

My greatest fear was that one day Luska would rule the world. And he was right: with this, he could.

"Let's get home. We have a wedding to attend tomorrow," Maxim told me and then began to walk. My legs moved against my will to follow him.

A wedding. Tomorrow. To Maxim Vlek. I could think of nothing worse.

CHAPTER TWENTY-SIX

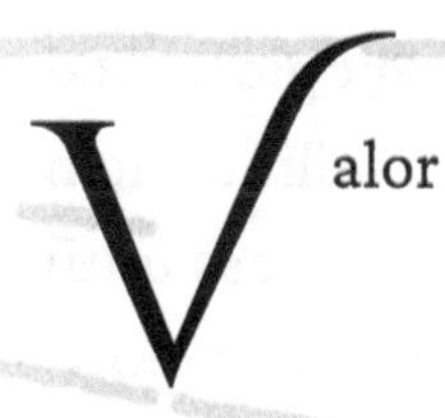

alor

I HAD A NEW MOTTO. *What would Aisling do?* It was how I was handling everything so fast. I'd convinced the admirals to allow my plan to detonate a bomb over the Luskin army base off their west coast. We'd spent all day and night evacuating our people. They took trains and cars and crossed into the Wilds on foot, into the barren, burned-out lands of Imbria—all evidence of the destruction we'd caused.

When they questioned why in the world they would go into enemy territory, I decided to steer from the *What Would Aisling Do?* territory and did what Valor would do. I told them the truth about Father—that we'd recently found out he was behind the attack that caused the Great Blackout and that the Imbrians were, in fact, our allies; Luska had a bomb that could level Riverine, and we needed to get out now and ask questions later. I told them that my sisters and I were different from our father; we would never turn on our own people, and deciding to tell the truth was evidence that we wanted things to run differently this time.

Some hesitated at my confession, but most people packed up and left with a simple three-day pack because we all knew that if Luska did have something that could take out Riverine, they would. My head was still firmly attached to my shoulders, so I was counting that as a win.

Some chose to stay at their own peril. People asked where my sister was, and again, I was honest in telling them Victory had been kidnapped and I was interim empress until Aisling returned with her on a rescue mission. It was a glorified truth, one I hoped was real and would end with both of my sisters alive and back home.

The good thing about gossip was that when you wanted something to spread like wildfire, it did. By the time I reached Evergreen, people were already on the move to Imbria and had heard the worst of the news. I overheard one family saying they always knew Father was a rotten liar and suspected him of dark deeds but thought Aisling and my sisters would turn the empire around. That was a relief. The risk of outing what my father did was a great danger to my sisters and me. But I wasn't sure how to get them to trust Kohen and Imbria otherwise, and to be honest, I couldn't sleep another day with the injustice of Ravi Badshah going down for something Father did. If the empire fell because of it, then so be it.

It was four in the morning by the time I made it back to the willow tree house I once shared with my sisters. Kohen was with me; half a dozen Fleet members patrolled outside. I had to meet Charlene and the other Talanagi bonded in about four hours in Emberlane Park to go over the plan and decide exactly how we would pull it off. Meanwhile, the admirals were having a bomb made with as many explosives as we had on hand in Riverine. Tetra had taken some time to get her mom to safety and was meeting me at the park in the morning. Liana had helped all night to ferry over people in need and promised to also meet in the park in the morning.

"You can sleep in my sister's room," I told Kohen and pointed to the door. He peered at the closed door with apprehension. "I'll just take the couch," he said.

I frowned. "Aisling won't care. And trust me, her bed is much better than that couch." If they were married, why was he being shy about sleeping in her bed?

Kohen swallowed hard. "Valor, if I smell her on that pillow, I'll never sleep."

My heart broke then. For the first time in my young life, I couldn't wait to one day fall in love—to have a man love me so much that they might be so affected by my smell.

"Got it," I said. My sister was super private, so she hadn't really told us about Kohen. When he'd said they married in secret earlier, my heart nearly stopped! But seeing him today, flying around with me and doing whatever needed to be done for the people of Amersea, I could see that his affection for my sister was genuine.

"Any more visions with the new plan?" I asked him hopefully.

He frowned. "No. Nothing."

I nodded. "Good."

He chuckled. "Good?"

"Yeah. It means you haven't had a vision saying we would fail. I'll take those odds. We're getting my sisters back," I declared.

He grinned, and it made him look so much hotter than his normal, grumpy, stoic face. I could see what my sister saw in him, and it made me think of Arjun. They looked so much alike.

"You're just like Aisling."

"I'll take that as a compliment," I told him.

He nodded seriously. "You should. Goodnight, Valor." He plopped onto the couch and sighed.

"Good night, Kohen." I walked back to my room and face-planted on the bed, passing out in seconds with my boots on. My last thought was that this must really be what it feels like to be empress: complete and total exhaustion.

CHAPTER TWENTY-SEVEN

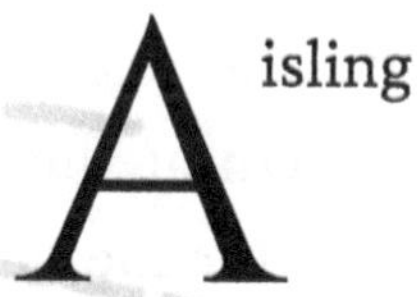

isling

My worst fear was realized when, after dinner, Maxim showed me to "our" room.

"But we're not married yet," I told him, searching for any way to head this off. The only saving grace was that Ricov had retired to another room with Whitney, and I was alone with my thoughts. They seemed to be keeping us in pairs.

Maxim unbuttoned his shirt, rolling his eyes. "I care not for propriety or your honor, but if you want to wait one more night before we begin to make heirs, it makes no difference to me."

Begin to make heirs made bile rise up in my throat. His

pants came off next, and I turned, giving him my back. I didn't like how casual he was being. This wasn't how it was done. My heart hammered in my chest as I fought for a reason to get alone and read the note Whitney had shoved in my pocket. I suspected Maxim had to stay in close proximity to me in order to use my power; that's why we were sharing a room. He'd posted two guards at the door and two at the window and made sure I knew it. There was no leaving this room.

"Can I have some private time in the bathroom?" I asked him.

"That's fine, but remember, I can control everything you do. So be a good girl," he taunted.

I nodded, walking across the room and into the bathroom. I shut the door behind me and glanced down at the folded women's pajamas that some maid had left for me. I didn't want to get into them. I didn't want to wear anything from him. I missed Kohen and Elaine and home.

I got undressed and ran the bath water quickly, splashing my face and soaping my body, skipping washing my hair. Then, I quickly opened my bond to Liana.

'I can talk, but only for a minute,' I told her.

'Are you safe? I've been so worried.'

'I am, but Maxim is worse than we thought. He can take anyone's power from within his physical proximity. He controls me with my own power, and his right-hand man can read thoughts, which is why I can't contact you outside of right now.'

'He has no soul,' Liana agreed. *'But you will be happy to know that Elaine lives. She's safe with your sisters.'*

I nearly broke down right then and there at that news. *'And my people? Maxim wasn't bluffing about this weapon. I saw it make a crater in the forest... It blew me off my feet. He'll come for Riverine if I don't hand it over.'*

'Your people have decided to trust Valor. They have been evacuating all day and will continue into the night.'

Valor? I thought Kohen and the admirals would have been heading up the evacuations.

'Valor has shown great responsibility and leadership. She told the people the truth, and they have seen a new generation in her —in you and all your sisters.'

The truth? My gut sank. *'She told them what my father did?'*

'Yes. And they still follow her to safety.'

Relief settled over me. If I did die here, or worse, had to live in the situation forever, at least my people would follow Valor, and Kohen's father was vindicated. It was good news.

'I should go.' I didn't want Maxim to get upset, and I still had to read the letter Whitney had furiously scribbled. I drained the tub and dried off quickly.

'Aisling, they are trying to find a way to rescue you both. Don't give up hope.'

I tried to feel any level of excitement about that, but I couldn't. I knew Kohen hadn't seen any reality in which I was free from Maxim and alive.

'Okay,' I said and then paused before shutting down the bond. *'Tell Kohen I love him and that if they can't rescue us, it's okay. Tell him to move on and just... be happy,'* I said as a tear fell down my cheek. I imagined Kohen married to Anika with children and no drama. That was probably what he needed.

'Aisling—'

'Goodbye, Liana.' I shut down the bond.

"Almost done in there?" Maxim asked.

"Yeah, I just have to go to the bathroom," I told him, and grabbed my dirty clothes, slipping them back on as I stepped into the smaller toilet room, shutting the door behind me and pulling out Whitney's note. There was no time to dwell on my sadness about the future I might have had with Kohen. The second I read the first line, that all washed out of my head. The handwriting was shaky, but the words were powerful.

I'M TAKING my sister tonight. I've been planning our escape for weeks, but now that I've seen you and your sister, I will take her with me, too. I cannot bear to see an innocent child used as a pawn in a war game. I will kill Ricov, and we will all flee to Amersea and plead for sanctuary. I'm assuming since I have the heir of the empress, they will grant it. I wish I could do more for you, but with Maxim's new power to control people, I cannot get close to him. I'm sorry. You're on your own. May God bless you and keep you, and may you take comfort in knowing your sister will be safe.

- W

TEARS ROLLED down my face onto the page and I nodded, smiling. The Luskins believed in one God, one being who looked down on everyone and guided them, and at this moment, it was a comforting idea to me. To know that my sister would be taken away from here was the only thing I could ever hope for.

A loud bang came at the door, and I jumped in alarm, crumpling up the note quickly and dropping it into the toilet, flushing it down.

"What are you doing in there?" Maxim's voice was right outside the door, which meant he'd breached the other bathroom door. I'd been so caught up in reading the letter that I didn't hear it. I made sure the note had flushed and then wiped my cheeks, opening the door and coming face to face with him.

"Relieving myself," I said flatly.

He skeptically ran his gaze all over me before resting on my shirt. "Why didn't you change?"

He was standing before me shirtless, in low-slung pajama pants. In another world, I'd say his body was fit and attractive, but I was so repulsed by the obvious evil in him I felt sick just looking at him.

"I feel more comfortable in my clothes."

He rolled his eyes, and I felt his power—my power—slide over me. One second, I was standing with my arms at my side, and the next, I was pulling my t-shirt over my head and standing before him in my bra. "You bastard," I spat as he made me reach for the button of my pants.

He grinned. "You should have worn the clothes I so graciously had made for you."

I unzipped my pants and watched as he let his gaze

linger over my underwear while I dropped my trousers to the floor.

I felt a wild rage rise up inside of me. Smoke began to simmer off the skin on my arms.

"Stop it," he growled, and I pushed against his command. I was standing in my bra and underwear against my will, and all I could think about was ripping his head from his body.

The smoke didn't stop, and Maxim's eyes widened. "Stop!" He lashed out, and I felt the power like a physical slap. The smoke fell away, leaving me breathless, and Maxim gave me his back. "Get dressed and come to bed. Tomorrow, we wed, and I become ruler of Amersea."

My stomach tied into knots. Based on Whitney's letter, it was probably best to keep Maxim calm, and in this room. If she had some big plan to escape tonight, the best thing I could do was make sure Maxim was asleep.

"Okay," I said quietly, and then picked up the pajamas and put them on. I walked out of the bedroom to find him watching me in a way that made the hairs on the back of my neck stand up.

I spied a couch against the far wall and began walking toward it. "I'll sleep there," I said, but my legs glued to the hardwood floor halfway there.

"You'll sleep with me in the bed," he commanded. My body turned against my will, and I began to walk towards the bed. I stared at him, trying to stifle my panic.

"I'd rather not. I'm old-fashioned," I lied.

His gaze narrowed as if he didn't believe me. "You've

deprived me of my sister, which means I need an heir as soon as possible. I've changed my mind about waiting. I don't see the harm in trying now." He again looked at my body in a way that caused me to panic, my mind struggling to find a reason to wait. I needed to keep everything calm so that Whitney could get away with Victory.

"Maxim?" I said his name in a sweet tone.

His gaze snapped up to my face with curiosity.

"I've come to terms with my new life here. As your wife. But I'd like to keep some of my culture and way of doing things. It would mean a lot to me if we could wait to share this bed until we were officially married. Please?" I put some extra syrupy-sweet inflection in my tone.

He said nothing. He just stared at me for an agonizingly long moment until, finally, he waved me off. "Fine. Sleep on the couch. I'm tired anyway." And with that, my legs were unglued, and I hurried to the couch and yanked the blanket off, throwing it over myself and giving him my back.

I'd bought myself one night. Tomorrow, I wouldn't be so lucky.

CHAPTER

TWENTY-EIGHT

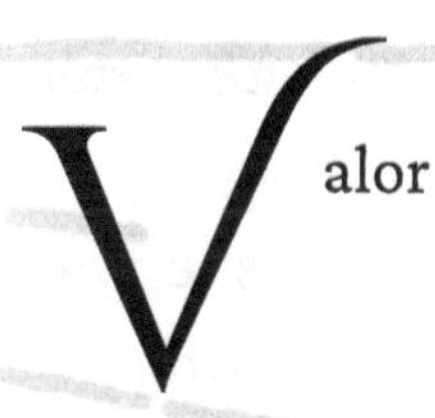

alor

KOHEN SHOOK me awake after only three hours of sleep, and we had a quick breakfast together.

"Any new visions about my plan?" I asked as we prepared to leave the house and go meet Charlene and the others at Emberlane Park.

"No," he said, sounding slightly terrified.

I nodded. "I think you've become too dependent on knowing the outcome. It's paralyzed you from acting."

He stilled at the front door and peered down at me. "Hmm, that was a wise observation for a fourteen-year-old."

I rolled my eyes. "*Almost* fifteen-year-old *empresssss.*" I let the word drag out to emphasize its importance.

Kohen smiled down at me, and I smiled back. I never had a brother, but I felt like if I did, it would be like this. When Kohen opened the door, I was surprised to see Liana standing next to Onyx and Zara. All three seemed to be deep in conversation, facing each other and peering into one another's eyes.

"What's going on?" I asked.

Zara looked over at me. *'Liana wants to be the one to fly you on the mission. She's got more training, and if it goes wrong, she's better suited to get you home safely.'* I could feel the hurt in her voice as she said, *'And I agree. I'll go to Imbria to be with Virtue so that I can protect her if need be.'*

Liana dipped her head in respect as if saying she was agreeing with this plan. I liked her, and I wanted to bring my sister home, so I nodded. *'Okay.'*

Walking over to Zara, I hugged her neck, stroking the scales there. Being young sucked sometimes. People underestimated you and thought you couldn't do stuff. But I knew my sister's creature was a badass, and so I would defer to her lead since I knew Aisling would want me to.

Kohen nodded as if Onyx had told him everything and he was on board. Liana and Onyx had a special bond. I knew they spoke to each other and shared almost everything.

Zara gave me one last goodbye and then flew off into the morning sun as Kohen and I took the short flight to Emberlane Park. Liana was bigger than Zara and a smoother flier, too, so I didn't have to struggle to hold on. She was fitted with a saddle, which we hadn't had time to do for Zara yet. Peering at my sister's well-worn saddle, I found myself missing her badly. Our world had changed so much in such a short time that I had no idea what the future would look like, even after we brought Aisling home. It felt like nothing would ever be the same again, but if I could at least get all of us together, then everything would be alright.

When we landed in Emberlane Park, I noticed Elaine leaning on her cane next to Tetra.

"Elaine!" I slipped off of Liana and ran to her, trying not to crush her when I hugged her. My throat tightened with emotion when she squeezed me back, and the scent of her coconut lavender shampoo washed over me. Elaine would always be like a mother to me and my sisters. Almost losing her nearly broke me.

"How did you get here?" I asked when we finally pulled away, and Tetra gave me a hug as well. It was weird to see Tetra without her cane. I still hadn't fully processed my gift and its repercussions.

"Liana flew me in," Elaine said as she stood next to Tetra. "If you are planning an Aisling and Victory rescue, I want to be a part of planning it."

I nodded. "Then you will be."

Admiral Caruso walked over with her creature beside her, a clipboard in her hand. There were deep bags under her eyes. She didn't look like she'd slept at all. "The evacuation is going well. By sundown, everyone who has agreed to leave should be gone." She looked at Kohen. "The Imbrians have been more than accommodating. Thank you."

He nodded. "Of course. We don't have much, but what we do have is yours."

The admiral's eyes grew misty. She cleared her throat and nodded. "The payload took all night, but my men are flying it in now."

"Flying?" I asked.

She pointed to the sky, where I saw a blue griffin carrying a large box hanging from a rope in its claws.

"Lieutenant Colt will be going with you. Recently bonded to a Talanagi. He will be leading the mission since he's the only one of you who is actually in the Fleet and has gone through military training."

Ouch. Okay, that was true, though.

Colt landed, and then one by one, so did Charlene and the other newly bonded, fresh-out-of-the Wilds cadets.

Everyone looked at me as if expecting a speech, and I paled. I hadn't prepared anything, and honestly, I had no idea what to say. That was my sister's thing. I peered at Elaine in panic, and she nodded once.

Elaine cleared her throat. "Thank you all for answering the call in Amersea's greatest time of need. Our empress and one of her heirs has been taken captive by Luska..."

The dozen or so people surrounding us growled their indignation.

"...but you are not yet trained, and this will be a dangerous mission, so I know Aisling would not want this to be forced upon you. If any of you feel that you do not want to participate, there is no shame in flying on to Imbria and helping the evacuation."

No one said a word, and pride swelled in my chest.

Elaine nodded. "Very well, then. Here's what I think you should do."

Thirty minutes later, we had a solid plan. Elaine had two Luskin uniforms that were pulled off the dead bodies from our car attack. Two of the people in our group would wear them and fly ahead, tricking the initial spotters. We would trail behind with the payload, with Tetra protecting us, and drop it as close as we could to their base. Elaine emphasized that we weren't actually trying to take out their base. We were trying to make the capital city think an all-out attack was happening and draw them east to give Kohen time to sneak into Luska from the west. If we did hit their base dead-on, great, but the object was to just get close while also staying safe.

Some in our group had discovered fire-throwing powers and wind control, and others didn't know what they had. We were all bringing bolt shooters and hoping for the best in an air assault with the Luskin army.

Tetra wanted us to fly in close formation, as her shield power could only stretch so far. She'd ride with me on Liana.

By the time we'd run over the plan at least ten times and accounted for every possibility, it was lunchtime, and Kohen was ready to begin his journey to the Wilds. We would be leaving shortly after, with the aim of dropping the bomb at sundown. He decided to have Onyx fly him to the Wall, and then they would both go on foot through the Wilds, avoiding the skies, so he was leaving early.

I could tell he was nervous. He got quiet and kept

fiddling with something at his waist. When it was time for him to head out, he called me over to talk privately.

"I've never done something big like this without seeing the outcome. If I die trying to rescue Aisling, I can think of no greater way to go."

My heart twisted in my chest. It was the most romantic thing I'd ever heard.

I grasped his shoulders and looked him in the eye. "I have faith in you, Kohen. Bring my sisters home." I pulled him in for a hug.

His arms wrapped around me, and he squeezed tightly before pulling away. Something about my words seemed to have an effect on him because he looked more confident. He nodded and slipped onto Onyx's back.

"You make a great little empress," he said.

"Little?" I scoffed with one hand on my hip, and he grinned, kicking off the ground and heading for the sky.

I never thought I would say it, but I loved a Badshah—not in the romantic way, but in the brotherly way. I mean, my sister technically married him, so he was my brother now, right? Something about Kohen Badshah and his unyielding loyalty to my sister's happiness had won me over. He could do no wrong in my eyes at this point.

I turned and walked over to the small group of newly minted, untrained soldiers that I hoped were going to help save my sister's life.

Stars have mercy on us.

CHAPTER TWENTY-NINE

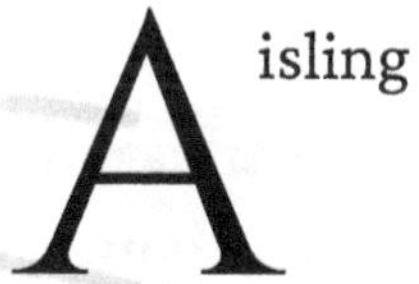

isling

I WAS awoken by a banging on the door. Sitting bolt upright, I forgot where I was for a second until I saw Maxim traipse across the bedroom and open it. Then, the horror of my reality came rushing back to me. I had meant to stay awake all night and make sure Maxim didn't come near me, but I'd fallen asleep.

"What is it?!" he snapped. The sky was still dark, the sun just barely coming up.

"Ricov is dead. His body is cold. Whitney and the two girls are missing. I estimate she has a five-to-seven-hour lead," a male voice I didn't recognize informed Maxim.

"WHAT!?" Maxim roared in the scariest timbre I'd ever heard from a human. My legs involuntarily launched me out of bed. I was standing before him as he breathed down my face.

"Do you know anything about this?" he said.

I couldn't help the grin that spread across my lips. My sister was gone. *Safe.* It was game over. Maxim wasn't getting nice, play-by-the-rules-Aisling anymore.

He slapped me hard across the face but kept my body frozen to the spot so I couldn't even shy away from the hit. I just took it full-on. Pain exploded behind my eyes as they instantly watered, and for some crazy reason, I laughed.

Maxim's eyes widened in fury. "What's so funny?" he roared.

"You hit like my little sister," I taunted, no longer caring about pleasing him. Now that I knew Whitney had gotten my sister out, I'd spend the rest of my life messing with Maxim.

I had about two seconds to regret that choice of words before he balled his hand into a fist and cracked me on the side of the head so hard that everything went black.

I CAME to shortly after with a screaming Maxim and a headache. He was now fully dressed, and I was in his bed with a maid of some sort, looking fearfully at me. From the doorway, Maxim was barking orders for Whitney and my sister to be found. When he was done, he glared at the maid.

"Get her ready. Our wedding is in three hours. Set up in my office. I have to get work done. And bring our lunch there." All of a sudden, I was getting out of bed. My head screamed when Maxim forced me to stand, but I ignored it. As I passed a mirror, I was startled by the black eye and cut above my cheek. Lunch? How long was I out?

Maxim was very telling by having me come to his office to get ready for our sham wedding so that he could get work done. It told me there *were* limits to his power, and that was close proximity. How close? I had no idea. Was it ten feet? A hundred? How fast could I run so that I could take back my power and then use it on him to make him cut his own throat? Only one way to find out. And with my sister gone, I had nothing to lose.

The second we reached the hallway and Maxim went left, I went right, bolting into the fastest run of my life. I got about four feet when my legs froze, and I came tumbling down to the floor, landing hard on my shoulder. I lay on my side as the eerily slow footsteps of Maxim came nearer. He loomed over me, saying nothing for a terrifying amount of time. Finally, he crouched down, cocking his head to the side. "I've heard the rumors. I know you can be reborn if you die, but if you continue to disobey me, I will make sure to keep you alive and in just enough pain to wish you were dead."

My heart sank. Maxim was slowly breaking my fiery spirit. I wasn't scared of pain. I was an Everhart. But continued torture would eventually break me, no matter how strong I was. Was it even worth the fight? Maxim hauled me up by the armpit and then animated my legs to follow him.

As we walked, Maxim leaned into my ear. "Now that you've shown me this side of you, I'll have to make sure you never run again, little pet. I hope you like living on a leash."

Liana was right. He was evil.

As I had that thought, I was reminded that Ricov was dead and so my thoughts were truly my own again. Opening the bond, I felt Liana burst into my mind. *'Tell me how you are!'* she said.

'A Luskin defector named Whitney broke free with Victory and her sister,' I told her quickly. *'They should be in Amersea soon. They've been traveling on foot all night. She has an eagle creature. Make sure she is treated with trust and respect. Give them both asylum.'*

I could feel her excitement at the news. *'I will make sure the admirals know and have soldiers on the lookout. We have a plan to get you back, Aisling. Just hold on.'*

I said nothing. Hope was a dangerous thing in my situation. *'I have to go,'* I lied. *'But I'll keep the bond open if I can.'* I had no idea if Maxim had anyone else around who could read minds. *'Don't tell me anything specific. Maxim could be listening. I have no idea.'*

'I love you, young one. We will get through this.' I could physically feel her heartache through our bond.

'As long as my sisters are safe, I can get through anything.'

'Just hold on a little longer,' she repeated.

'I gotta go,' I said again, and then Maxim opened the door to his office.

I sat in a chair off to the side, and over the next hour, I was dolled up with makeup to cover my bruises, curls in my hair, and all the fake things to trick people into thinking I was willingly about to marry Maxim.

The entire time, only one man was on my mind, one pair of lips, one heart, one soul.

Kohen Badshah.

CHAPTER

THIRTY

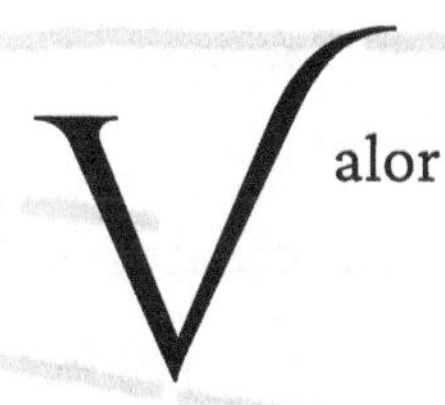

Valor

WE'D FLOWN ALL DAY, and now the sun was setting, and I could see the Luskin peninsula coming into view. Tetra had a shield around the twelve of us, flying in a close circle. The two we'd chosen to pretend to be Luskin soldiers, Charlene and Colt, had gone ahead of us. I hoped Kohen had made it into the Wilds by now and was ready to make his way to the Luskin capital. He would be able to fly and make good time with Onyx once we drew their forces west. Right as we'd been about to leave, Liana had received a message from Aisling that Victory was on her way back with some Luskin defectors. I told the admirals, but I wasn't able to stay and make sure she was okay. We had to keep to our schedule, and it was all converging at this moment. Liana held the payload between her claws as we moved from being over the water to Luskin land. I saw a building up ahead with a large wall that could be a military base, but it was hard to say because we were too far.

Ahead of us, Charlene and Colt were dots. Two other dots wearing Luskin red were racing up from the ground to meet them in the air.

This is it!

"Get ready!" I called out to everyone.

There was an exchange of fire in the air, and then two bodies sank from their creatures like stones. I squinted, relieved to see that it wasn't Charlene or Colt.

"Fly fast now!" I told our group, and their creatures flapped their wings like mad. Much closer now, I was able to confirm that it was indeed their western base, and over two dozen soldiers with flying Talanagi were now rising on their creatures to meet us.

"I've got you!" Tetra said, and I could see a shimmery shield in front of us as Charlene and Colt were flying back to get into her protection. Once they were inside, it was mayhem. The soldiers threw wind, fire, and arrows at Tetra's shield as we made our way towards their base. I knew we didn't need to send the bomb directly over their base, but it would be nice.

Tetra's shield wobbled. She'd warned us that she was still refining her gift and that she might, at some point, lose it. We were ready for that.

"Positions!" I cried.

We were almost directly over their base! The truth was, I wanted to blow their base sky high for what they did to my sisters.

Our fire throwers got in front of our group, and we all raised our bolt shooters.

"It's going!" Tetra cried out just as her shield dropped.

The moment it was gone, we pummeled them with what fire and arrows and wind we could, blowing riders off of their creatures, and I peered down to see we were over their base.

"Now, Liana!" I cried in joy as she let go of the payload. I watched as it fell to the earth. Hundreds of soldiers scrambled like scattering ants, but they were too slow. The bomb exploded, taking out anyone in the vicinity on the ground. Everyone in our group whooped and hollered as the other Luskin soldiers left us to return to base and help. I thought I would feel a triumphant joy as I looked down on the carnage of a job well done—of Luskins killed. But instead, I felt numb inside. They killed us. We killed them. Back and forth until the end of time. Would this war ever end?

I sat back, dropping a little as Tetra leaned into my ear. "What's wrong, Val? We did it!"

"We did what? We killed hundreds of people."

Tetra's face grew serious. "They have your sister. Doing stars-knows-what with her. We had to do this."

I nodded. Maybe this time we did. But the others? The decades of war... did we have to do that? I felt sick the entire race home. All I could do was pray we'd given Kohen time to get in and get my sister unnoticed. I was ready for Aisling to be in charge, for her to be the one who was responsible for all the deaths. I wasn't cut out for this, I realized. Leading people felt great, but killing them wasn't something I wanted to do ever again. I knew it was very un-Everhart of me to say, but I was done with war and killing. I wanted peace.

CHAPTER
THIRTY-ONE

Aisling

IT FELT like an out-of-body experience walking down the aisle with Maxim as the sun set on the horizon. I'd fought him again, and he'd taken full control of my body, even my tongue. I was gagged, cemented in whatever shape he wanted me. I walked with a military posture, jaw clenched shut as I screamed a guttural wail from my closed throat. The onlookers, about a hundred in all, watched in a mixture of mild fascination and horror as Maxim and I met the priest at the end of the aisle. I wore a stupid white Luskin dress, and I hated everything about this moment, but nothing as much as the stack of papers waiting for me at the end of the aisle.

As we reached the end, I peered down to see the words *Surrender of Amersea to Luska*, and I felt like I was going to throw up.

No, no, no. Not like this. This wasn't even a peace treaty where we both agreed to stop fighting. This was me giving a madman ownership of my country.

I screamed louder, but because Maxim had frozen my tongue and jaw, it was just an animalistic, garbled wail. I wanted to trigger him. I wanted his people to see what a psycho he really was.

And it worked. Maxim's hand snaked out and wrapped around my throat, pinching off all sounds along with airflow.

"Shut *up*. Let's get this over with," he growled.

The priest looked uncomfortable, but I peered around to see a few men in the front row wearing red Luskin soldier uniforms who were grinning. Everyone else appeared in shock at Maxim's behavior. *Good.*

When he let go, I gasped for breath through my nostrils, my jaw still clamped shut.

Maxim looked at the priest. "I want this done in sixty seconds. Make it legal."

The priest nodded fearfully. "We are gathered here to witness Aisling Everhart's surrender of Amersea to Luska by her legal marriage to Maxim Vlek. Under Luskin law, when a woman marries a man, her possessions become his possessions."

I snorted, and Maxim glared at me. Well, *that* was a convenient law. Everything made sense now! I knew now why Kohen had us marry first, other than being in love. It meant that this truly wasn't a legal wedding. I felt a grin trying to tug at my lips.

"By signing this agreement, you enter into a lifelong marriage, and Aisling's possessions, including her rulership, pass to Prime Leader Maxim."

Everyone clapped loudly, but I could see their eyes bugging in shock; the clapping was too coordinated. He was forcing them.

"Sign here." The priest handed Maxim a pen.

He grinned and leaned forward, signing the document. Then he handed me the pen. I tried with everything I had to fight him, but my stupid traitorous arm snaked out and grasped the pen. In that moment, a wild hope came over me and I scanned the crowd and the fields behind them, praying Kohen would jump out and save me from this fate. But as my hand came down on the paper and I signed my name, my fate was sealed. Though this wedding might not be legal, it was happening whether I wanted it to or not.

The crowd clapped again.

"By the power I carry as a priest of the high church of Luska, I grant this marriage," the priest said quickly. Then I was walking again, following Maxim out of there. The crowd stood, seeing us off, as Maxim and I walked over to the two generals wearing Luskin uniforms. "I have what I need now. Take Amersea."

Take Amersea. Those words were like an arrow to the heart.

"Lord, we've lost Sergeant Whitney. We have no activated bombs."

Maxim shoved the papers into one of the men's chests until they caught it. "You have this. Bring me my bounty by morning, or you're fired."

Maxim then walked angrily away, and I scurried after him against my will. Take Amersea by morning? Stars, had my people had enough time to flee?

'Liana, they're attacking tonight. Make sure Riverine is empty.'

'We just blew up their western base,' Liana said. *'Hold on.'*

Surprise rushed through me at her words. She blew up their western base?

'It's too late. We're married. I married Maxim and signed away all my rights to Amersea.' Whether it was truly legal or not, it was done. The papers were signed in front of a hundred people.

'Did Kohen have a new vision? Did he see us both making it out of this alive?' I asked as hope began to beat in my heart.

'Just hold on,' Liana said again, and my hopes were dashed.

If Kohen died trying to rescue me, I'd never forgive myself.

'Liana, tell him not to come unless he's sure!' I told her frantically as Maxim forced me back towards the house after him like the loyal little pet I was.

But Liana didn't answer, and I knew then that my sweet,

protective Kohen would risk his life for even a chance at saving me. If I had to mourn the love of my life and live as Maxim's slave forever, then my heart would never recover.

Just as we were stepping up onto the back porch, a uniformed soldier came running toward us. "Prime Leader!" he called. There was a handheld radio in his palm, and he was wide-eyed. "Grigov Base has been hit, a direct hit by the Amerseans!"

Maxim froze, and my heart beat wildly.

"What?" he asked in a deadly calm, his gaze flicking to me.

"Sir, they had two dozen Talanagi. Dropped a large payload on the base. We're still getting a body count. We think they are coming back with more. In retaliation for..." The soldier's gaze fell to me.

Two dozen. Charlene and the new cadets pulled that off? *Incredible.*

Maxim released my facial muscles, and I grinned.

"Tell me what you know of this," he commanded me.

For a wild second, I thought he actually had the power to force me to tell him the truth, but nothing came out of my mouth.

"Tell me!" he bellowed.

I stayed silent with a half-cocked smirk.

He turned back to the soldier. "Send all available troops west. Kill any Amerseans on sight."

My gut clenched when he said that. Charlene and... Valor weren't there, was she?

'Liana, get everyone out of there. They are sending all troops

your way,' I told her as Maxim grasped me by the back of my hair and the sky filled with flying Talanagi heading west.

'Don't worry, we are.'

Maxim snapped his fingers and then his wolf was there. I'd forgotten about the creature since he rarely had them around, not like others who stuck close to their bonded. "Walk this perimeter all night long and warn me if you suspect anything," he told the wolf, and it took off.

He peered up into the sky at his firebird and obviously gave her some instructions because she flew off as well.

"They think they are going to take you from me?" he asked me. "Your people are my people now. *You* are mine now," he growled.

I thought he might call a strategy meeting with all of his leaders. That's what I would do, but no, he rushed us inside the house while the guests left the "wedding" and then he locked all the doors and told the staff to not allow anyone in. He wasn't a leader. His generals were leading without his direct command. He was a coward. A boy *playing* at being a leader.

We ate dinner together in absolute silence as I watched his nervous tics play out. Eyes darting from the window to the door. Pursing lips. Picking nails.

When someone finally knocked, he actually jumped up, and I laughed. Suddenly, my hand grasped the steak knife beside me unbidden, and I held it to my own throat. Maxim held my gaze.

Go ahead and kill me, bastard. I'll come back in three days and make you wish you were never born, I wanted to say. But thought better of it. The truth was Maxim was unhinged, and that scared me.

At the door, the soldier whispered something in his ear. The entire time, the knife was pressed to my throat. When the soldier left, he shut the door and walked over to me. I finally released the knife, dropping it to the floor. He had me stand, knocking the chair over with how fast I'd moved, and then I was pressing my body up against his, leaning into his mouth.

"Don't," I growled, and then his lips were on mine.

Bile rose in my throat as I fought the kiss, fought the control. I hated myself for not being able to move, hated myself for kissing him back with my body but not with my heart.

After a moment, he pulled back, grinning.

"I am ready to consummate our marriage now. In the morning, we will go stay in my country house while all of this blows over."

I opened my mouth to speak, to tell him to eat razor blades and die, but he clamped my jaw shut.

He walked from the room, and I followed him, one leg in front of the other while I was screaming inside.

'Liana! I—' I didn't know what to say. *'I'm losing hope,'* I told her honestly. *'I need good news.'*

Liana's energy washed over me, strong and motherly then. *'We just got back. Victory is here with the defectors. She made it. Victory is safe!'*

Tears built in my eyes, and joy flooded my heart. She was safe. It was all worth it because Victory got out and was safe.

Okay. I could endure anything if it meant my sisters were safe. Even the unthinkable.

'I love you,' I told her. *'I'm going to close the bond now.'*

'Aisling, wait. Kohen is—'

I shut the bond, not wanting her to witness what I was about to go through, and then Maxim opened his bedroom door. He walked inside, and I followed, shutting the door behind me as he commanded. I walked past him and over to the bed as he forced my limbs to move. His back was still to the door as he watched me take off my clothes.

"Get on your knees," he commanded, and I fell to my knees before him, tears streaming down my face. I looked up. And when I did, I nearly screamed. Above his head, hiding in the rafters, were a pair of striking blue eyes.

Kohen.

I saw Kohen at the same time Maxim must have sensed him because he craned his neck to look up just as the ear-splitting bang of the gun went off.

One second, Maxim was standing before me, looming over me, and the next, he was tipping over like a falling tree, his head blown open. For the first time in days, my body was my own. My hands shook as adrenaline rushed through me, and the door flew open.

Another shot. And another. Kohen killed two guards in rapid succession and then leaped from the ceiling and landed before me, placing his body in front of mine like a shield. Three more people came to the doorway and one to the window. Kohen shot them all with deadly precision.

They blinked out like lights, going from standing to completely without life within a second.

I was in shock. Everything happened very fast then. Kohen had to help me dress. I knew we didn't have much time before more people came, and I couldn't speak. I couldn't believe he was here. We crawled out the window together, and Maxim's wolf was dead outside the window. More soldiers approached us, and then two more shots went off.

Kohen was killing people from fifty feet away. It was incredible. We ran on foot to the thick woods by Maxim's house, and Onyx was there. I nearly wept with relief when I saw him. Kohen got me onto his back first, and then crawled on in front of me so that we were facing each other.

Kohen peered over at me. "Do you think you could use your power right now if we meet sky resistance?"

I wanted to say yes. I wanted to be a badass who wasn't affected by what I had just gone through, but instead of answering, I just burst into sobs.

Kohen crushed me to his chest, fully engulfing me in his strong arms.

"Onyx, avoid the sky. We're going on foot through the Wilds," he told her.

I broke down in the safety of the arms of the man I loved. Being controlled by a madman for two days, being forced against my will to marry him, kiss him, and almost...

"It's okay," Kohen whispered in my ear as Onyx walked through the forest as fast as he could. "Whatever happened with him is over now, and it doesn't change how I feel about you. Aisling, I love you, and I'm only sorry I didn't get there sooner."

His words were like a balm to my wounds, and I realized at that moment that no man had ever really loved me until now. Not my father, not Jace, not even Alek. Kohen was showing me what true love was, and instead of pushing it away or thinking I didn't deserve it, I was going to lean into it. I was going to hold tightly to it and cherish it forever.

"I married him. I signed over Amersea," I told him shakily.

Kohen smiled then. "I had a vision not five minutes before I reached you. Luksa signs a peace treaty now that Maxim is dead and your marriage wasn't valid."

Hope burst to life in my chest. "They do?"

He nodded. "No one wants war anymore, my love. We all want to raise our children in peace."

I let him hold me as Onyx walked us all the way to the area where the Wall had been torn down to let Talanagi in. The place where it all began with Kohen and me.

As we crossed into Amersea, I looked into his eyes.

"Did you ever once just think, 'Wow, that girl is not worth what I'm going to have to go through to get her?'" I joked.

He stroked his finger over my bottom lip, sending shivers down my spine. "Not even once, my love."

I prayed then that every woman had a love like Kohen Badshah.

CHAPTER THIRTY-TWO

Aisling

KOHEN WAS RIGHT. The very next day we proposed a peace treaty between all of our nations and showed that Kohen and I had been legitimately married before Maxim forced me and that they had no claim to my lands. The Luskin leadership signed the peace treaty without hesitation, and the day officially marked the end of the war. Peace Day.

My people made their way back home to Amersea, grateful to find it still standing, and Kohen and I began to talk about plans to spend the summers in Amersea and the winters in Imbria.

We decided to build a new house in each place that

would fit our five siblings and future children. Arjun and Tej got along well with my sisters. We were one big, happy family. A little too happy, maybe, as I caught Arjun kissing Valor, and then we had to have a talk about rules and living under the same roof during puberty.

Two weeks after the peace treaty was signed, I was in the kitchen of Kohen's home in Imbria when I felt Liana pull at my attention.

'It's time,' she said, and a full-body chill broke out on my skin. I'd told Kohen about Liana's past, her daughters, the fire sky, and my fear that when I was settled, she might leave.

'No,' I told her. I dropped the knife I'd been holding and went outside.

Kohen just watched me but said nothing, which meant Onyx had already told him what was happening.

I went outside, and Liana was waiting.

'Time for what?' I asked, hoping I was just being paranoid.

'Come, let's take a flight. Our last flight.'

'No...' I sank to the ground, my heart shattering into a thousand pieces. She walked over to me, nuzzling my neck, and I clung to her like a small child would. *'Please don't do this. I need you. I still need you.'*

'You don't. Not as much as my other girls do. It's time.'

This wasn't happening. But I knew that if I didn't go with her, she'd just leave without me, and I didn't want that. I slipped onto her back and leaned forward, hugging her neck. *'What if they aren't alive anymore, or their life is fine and they don't need you, or you don't even make it?'*

I felt so selfish at that moment.

'What if it was Victory, Valor, and Virtue?' she asked.

That won the argument. She was right. These were her children, her grandmother, her whole world she'd left behind.

'I'm sorry. I don't want to be without you.'

'I know, young one. But we are bonded. No amount of distance can separate us.'

I didn't want to tell her this, but she didn't understand what this would do to me as empress to be creatureless. I'd have to succeed to Valor. But I would if it was what Liana wanted.

'You will not be creatureless,' she told me as she flew fast and hard for the Wilds.

'I know, but you won't be here, so people will see me as such.'

'I don't mean me. You will bond another. A dragon.'

'No. I don't want another! I want you.'

'You have me. Always. But you will have her, too.'

'Wait, how do you know I will bond another? Kohen had a vision?'

'Yes. He didn't know how to tell you I was leaving. He loves you too much to see you live in sadness.'

Oh, he would hear from me later about that!

'Maybe I can go with you. I can survive fire and be reborn. What if your world needs help? We can come back together with your daughters.'

'You cannot come, Aisling.'

'Why? We could try. Worst case, I am reborn, right?' I was frantically trying to think up ways not to lose her.

'Because you are pregnant.'

Her words nearly knocked me off her back.

'Did Kohen tell you that?'

'No. I see life energy, remember? I've known for a week. The baby would not survive rebirth, and my world has never seen a human. You would probably be killed. I'm sorry, Aisling, but this is the end of my time with you. And what a blessing it has been to be by your side.'

Pregnant? I placed my hand on my belly and couldn't help but grin. An heir of both Imbria and Amersea... it would be the first.

Before I knew it, Liana was descending over the Wilds. When she landed, she set me down on the forest floor, and I looked up into the fiery sky.

I hated goodbyes. I hated this. I slid off her back and clung to her neck.

'My life was made better because of you,' I told her.

'And mine because of you,' she replied.

I wiped away a stray tear and stepped back as movement at my back caused my head to turn that way.

Kohen was waiting off to the side with Onyx.

All the people who loved her and truly knew her were here to say goodbye.

"I hope you make it. I hope you find them. I'll never stop thinking about you," I said.

'I'll never forget when I had to explain to you that my eggs weren't fertilized,' she responded.

'Hey, we said we would never speak of that again!' I smiled, glad she was leaving on a lighthearted note.

'Goodbye, Aisling.'

'Goodbye,' I managed as my throat tightened with emotion.

Kohen came up behind me and wrapped his arms around me as we both watched her kick off the ground and shoot upwards like a fireball. We'd flown over and under the fire sky plenty of times but never *through* it. Watching Liana get closer and closer to the orange and pink fiery glow had my heart in my throat.

Come on, make it, I cheered in my head, holding Kohen's arms around me. Then it happened. She breached the fire; there was a flash of light, and then nothing, like she'd been sucked into space. She was gone.

I nodded, turning around in Kohen's arms. "You knew? And didn't tell me?"

He frowned. "I couldn't bear it. I'm sorry."

I nodded. "That's okay. I know something you don't know now, too." I grinned.

He cocked his head to the side. "What do you mean?"

I shrugged nonchalantly. "Oh, nothing. You will have to wait and see."

"Aisling, what is it?" He jabbed me with one finger in the ribs, and I laughed. "You'll see."

Pulling me into his arms, he peered down at me. "Marry me again?"

"What?" I laughed.

"Marry me in front of the entire country in the biggest wedding our people have ever seen."

I grinned. "Say it again."

"Marry me."

"No, say *our* people."

Leaning down, he kissed my mouth. "Our people."

It felt like the entire time I'd known Kohen, he'd been working to get me to see that the Imbrians and Amerseans were equals, united and better together, and I'd finally reached that place. I would die for Imbria, just as I would for Amersea, and I knew we still had some kinks to work out, but I was proud to call these people my own.

EPILOGUE

Four-ish years later
Aisling

I COULDN'T BELIEVE the triplets were nineteen today. It felt like a lifetime ago that I made the decision to send Valor into the Wilds to bond a Talanagi. Now both of my remaining sisters would go next month when the Lottery took place. We still held the Lottery even though the peace between Luska was strong. We never knew when war would come knocking at our door, and an heir of the empress must have a creature.

"Mama." Little Liana tugged at my jacket, and I peered down at her. She had bright blue eyes like her father, and dark hair, with a feisty personality that I'm pretty sure she got from me. I scooped her up into my arms and kissed her nose.

"Are you excited for the party?" I asked her.

"Yes. I want cake!" she screamed in my face, and I laughed.

"Someone called for cake?" Kohen walked into the kitchen, where I'd been setting up for the party, and my husband had never looked sexier. He was holding a cake and wearing our one-year-old son, Ravi, in a baby carrier on his chest.

Yum.

"Cake!" Liana screamed and bucked so ferociously from my arms that I nearly dropped her. I let her wriggle down from me; she ran to her father and nearly knocked him over. He was an expert at holding two bucking wild children. Setting the cake down, he picked her up, propping her on one hip as her brother snoozed in the baby carrier. We could afford a governess, and stars knew I considered it daily, but Kohen and I agreed we wanted to be the ones to raise our children. When we had state matters to attend to at the same time, with him being king of Imbria and me being empress of Amersea, we left the kids with Tetra or Elaine or one of their aunts and uncles. It truly took a village, but it worked out.

"Guess what?" Kohen told little Liana.

"What?" She leaned in conspiratorially.

"Aunt Tetra is outside and said if you ask her reallllly nicely, she will let you ride Ariyel."

Liana's eyes widened. She squirmed out of Kohen's grasp

and went to the back door, flinging it wide open before running out to where Tetra and Elaine were hanging decorations outside with Alek. I always thought Tetra would end up with Dev, but they broke up not soon after the war ended. About two years ago, Alek and Tetra were both given positions in the same building, and something naturally blossomed between them. She tried to fight it on account of him once being into me, but I told her I didn't care, and I didn't. There was no one I'd rather my bestie be with. Alek was an amazing guy. The way he looked at her now as she scooped little Liana into her arms and spun on her feet made my heart sing.

Kohen grinned. Walking over to the couch, he set Ravi down and took off the baby carrier while I strode over and shut the back door so the bugs didn't get in. We both met each other halfway in the kitchen, and he pulled me into his arms, planting a sexy smooch on my mouth that made my toes curl.

"Kohen Badshah, are you asking for a third?" I teased him.

His eyes went half-lidded. "Maybe I am." He kissed my ear and trailed his lips down my neck. Kohen and I took a while to shift from being leaders of a war-torn country to leaders of nations that were at peace. Commander Ledger was still a commander, but he was all but retired now. We retained our military but cut way back, putting fifty percent of the Fleet in reserve status. Now Kohen and I mostly focused on rebuilding, and mostly on the Imbrian side. We had social programs and schooling and worked to lead our society on a better path than it was before. But it was hard to believe we'd both been flying our creatures into battle a little over four years ago.

I pulled back and grasped the sides of Kohen's face, peering into his deep blue eyes. He was right. Our love had changed history. The uniting of our family houses brought peace between all peoples. Now, when you went to Emberlane Park, there were just as many Imbrians as Amerseans and the same with Nimra. My food spice tolerance was rising, and I even spoke Imbrian now. I remembered being on the bus after the Lottery all those years ago and judging Kohen for his family name.

"I love you, I love you, I love you," I told him. Pure joy filled my heart until the point of bursting. A huge grin broke out on Kohen's face. "Remember that time in the closet in the underground base at Sky Reach? When I said I'd had the best vision of us?"

I remembered. I nodded.

Kohen smiled. "It just happened. It was this moment. Little Liana and Ravi, you saying you love me. This beautiful life we have built. Peace between all nations. This is... *perfect*."

I smiled. "Maybe I *do* want a third."

Kohen grasped my lower back and tucked me into him, lowering his voice. "I only need five minutes."

I burst into laughter, letting him kiss my neck.

Valor's voice came from behind me. "Eww, gross, get a room!"

Virtue was next. "Remind me to knock next time. I need to wash my eyes out."

"I think it's sweet," Victory trilled.

Kohen and I broke apart, smiling as the triplets filed into the living room and immediately went to the couch to coo over a sleeping Ravi.

I peered outside, where little Liana was riding Ariyel, and then my gaze flicked to Clary. My new dragon creature was lovely, but she wasn't Liana. She had given me the power over the wind, which was nice. I hadn't heard from Liana since she left, though even now when I got really quiet and focused on my breathing, she was there inside of me.

Sometimes I went to the Wilds and looked up into the sky and thought I saw a flash of her feathers through the fire sky. Was she alive? Was she alone? Did she need me? I felt like she'd sacrificed so much to help me, and I'd just abandoned her.

One day, I hoped we'd meet again. Until then, I was focusing on being happy, which is what she'd want.

THE END

ABOUT LEIA STONE

Leia Stone is the USA Today bestselling author of multiple bestselling series including Matefinder and Wolf Girl. She's sold over three million books and her Fallen Academy series has been optioned for film. Her novels have been translated into multiple languages and she even dabbles in script writing.

Leia writes urban fantasy and paranormal romance with sassy kick-butt heroines and irresistible love interests. She lives in Spokane, WA with her husband and two children.

www.LeiaStone.com

JOIN THE FAN CLUB

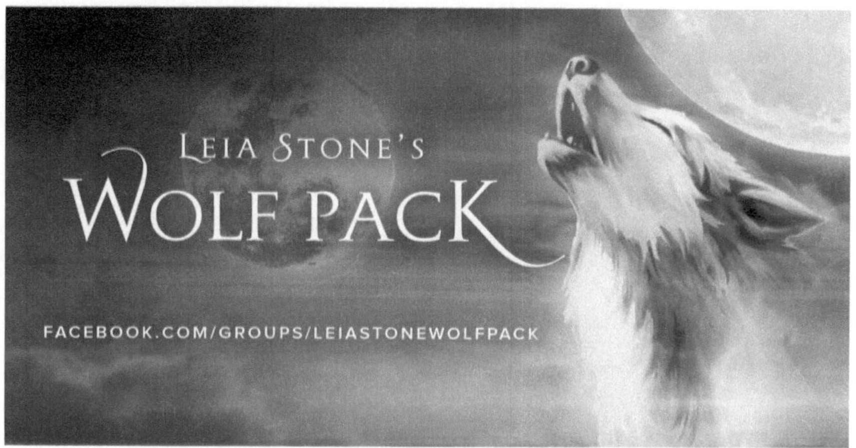

Get involved, make some friends, and get exclusive sneak peeks before anyone else.

News:

Also join my Newsletter! (Link on my website Leias tone.com) I only send one out when I have a new release or something exciting.

Shop:

Shop in my store! (LeiaStoneBooks.Com) I have special editions and ebook bundles and more!

 *Leia*

BOOKS BY LEIA STONE

SEE FULL LIST AT LEIASTONE.COM/BOOKS

Vampire Hunter Society

Shifter Island Series

Wolf Girl Series

Daughter of Light Series

The Titan's Saga

Supernatural Bounty Hunter Series

Dream Wars Series

Fallen Academy Series

Dragons & Druids Series

Matefinder Series

Matefinder: Next Generation

Hive Trilogy

NYC Mecca Series

Night War Saga

Water Realm Series

The Kings of Avalier Series

Gilded City Series

ACKNOWLEDGMENTS

To TikTok, which never made this or any of my books go viral. Thanks for nothing. (Kidding. Sort of.) To Brit Kings, my proofer, you are amazing. Thank you for fitting me in at the last minute and always making my babies shine. To Lee, my editor, a huge thank you, as always. To my family and my readers, I couldn't do this without your support! Thank you. Thank you. Thank you!

www.ingramcontent.com/pod-product-compliance
Lightning Source LLC
Chambersburg PA
CBHW020457310726
48979CB00016B/2692/J

* 9 7 8 1 9 5 1 5 7 8 5 1 0 *